SHOWDOWN IN DEVIL'S CANYON

Dee's .30-30 spat flame. The roar beat across the howling wind, echoing from canyon wall to canyon wall. Stratton's hat leaped, a sudden hole in its crown. And Mark Stratton leaped, too.

The wind down there on the canyon's floor had made the report seemingly come from the opposite canyon wall. Already Mark Stratton's .45 pointed upward. The saloonman shot at a boulder high on the southern slope of Devil's Canyon, and Dee was on the north slope.

Grinning devilishly, Dee took aim at Stratton's bootheel, stuck out behind him, the boot's toe digging for purchase in the sand. It was an impossible shot.

He squeezed the rifle's trigger.

The heel leaped from the boot.

Stratton leaped, too—straight upward. He pivoted, .45 pointing up at the hidden Dee. Lead whammed flint to ricochet madly into Wyoming space.

RIDE THE
WILD COUNTRY

Lee Floren

LEISURE BOOKS ∞ NEW YORK CITY

A LEISURE BOOK

Published by

Dorchester Publishing Co., Inc.
41 E. 60 St.
New York City

Printed in the United States of America

Chapter One

Although but an hour old, Round Rock's cowtown dance was in full swing. Fiddles squeaked. An accordion sobbed. Twenty-two year-old Dee Bowden suddenly stopped dancing with Nancy Craig.

Dee threw back his blond head. "Ride 'em, Cowboy!" he whooped.

Nancy put her hands over her ears. "Dee Bowden, please! You'll break my eardrums!"

"Hook 'em cow!"

"Dee, for heaven's sake—"

"I'm celebratin', Nancy. After all these years of waitin' the railroad has finally reached ol' Round Rock, Wyomin' Territory!"

All other dancers had stopped, also. Dee began a knee-lifting circular Sioux war-dance, high-heeled Justin boots pounding the Cowman's Hall's slivery soft-wood floor.

> I'm wild and wooly
>   And full of fleas,
> An' I've never been curried
>   Above my knees!

Dee looked up. Another young cowpuncher—a short waddy—was also dancing Sioux, knees lifting high, bootheels pounding. "My friend, Shorty Messenger," Dee said.

"My boss, Dee Bowden."

"My trusted hired hand," Dee said.

Shorty Messenger said, "Our night to howl!"

"I've got a black eye," Dee said. "Right eye. This afternoon in the rodeo, the stampede. Damned steer kicked me right in the eye. My top lip is swollen double size. Buckin' bronc pawed me."

"We're all crippled up," Shorty moaned. "My left leg. Bull kicked me. My right ear is torn loose a mite. Cayuse bit my ear. Whoopee. Long live Wyomin' an' Western Wyomin' Railroad!"

"Powder River!" Dee Bowden hollered. "A mile wide an' an inch deep."

"An' Gawd knows how long!" Shorty Messenger finished.

Dee stopped dancing Sioux. He grabbed Nancy around her thin waist. He immediately whirled her into a fast cowtown jig. "Sioux war-dance done," he said. "You're beautiful, Miss Craig!"

"You're not, Mister Bowden! Black eye! Swollen lip! Half drunk!"

"My old-time girl-friend," Dee moaned.

"And you are treating me very roughly, Dee Bowden. I should just walk off and leave you standing alone, in disgrace."

"Schoolteacher, how you talk!"

"I shouldn't even be dancing with you. My father—"

"I know all about your father." Dee looked about. Although most pioneers were tall men he was still taller. "Your father isn't here."

"He went home. About ten minutes ago."

"Drunk again?"

Anger stiffened Nancy Craig's lips. "You don't need to be so to the point, Dee Bowden! Yes, he was drunk—once again."

They danced in silence. They had known each other from grammar school days. Nancy had just returned from two years of college down in Cheyenne and would teach the first grade next year here in Round Rock.

School would begin next week.

Dee gave rough-and-tough Branch Craig some thought. Craig owned the biggest cow-spread in the Round Rock area, the Rafter V. He ran thousands and thousands of transplanted Texas longhorns over Wyoming grass, his dead father having trailed the longhorns up from Texas directly after the Civil War.

Nancy's mother had been killed a year before in a buggy runaway. Since then Branch Craig had turned to the bottle. Even Nancy—his only child—couldn't influence him.

"I'm worried," Nancy said.

Dee glanced down at her. "Over what?"

"My dad. He sold that trainload of prime steers today to that Chicago buyer. He got paid in cash."

"For the whole world to see, too," Dee Bowden said. "Railroad bigwigs even had a company photographer taking pictures of the money passing hands. Your dad put the money in Hendrick's bank, didn't he?"

"No, he didn't. That's what worries me."

Dee scowled. "You mean he's got all that money on him?"

"He has. And it runs into thousands."

"Why didn't he put it in Hendricks bank?"

"Oh, he and Hendricks had a quarrel today. Dad was drunk, as usual, and when drinking. Well, you know him. Belligerent and—oh, Dee, I am worried!"

"Who's ridin' with him?"

"He headed for home alone."

Dee's frown grew. "He'll get home all right. Don't you worry a bit, Nancy."

"And then you and he had that terrible quarrel— This afternoon, when you were calf-roping."

"I'm sorry about that, Nancy."

"Too late to be sorry. The words were said. What if Dad didn't drop that rope barrier as soon as you expected?"

7

"He deliberately held it up on me. The calf I was ropin' had already passed the barrier. Your father should have dropped the rope to let my horse through a full second ahead of time. I lost first money in ropin' because of him."

The argument had ben short, bitter, to the point. And in front of a few thousand spectators. Dee's hot young temper had flared. Branch Craig's middle-aged temper had broken loose.

Dee had threatened to hit the cowman. Craig had invited him to fisticuffs. Only physical intervention of rodeo contestants moving in had kept the two from matching fists.

"You've stole your last Rafter V cow, Bowden!" the rancher had stormed.

"Don't call me a cowthief!"

Finally, calmer heads had prevailed, but that had not been the first time Branch Craig had accused young Dee Bowden of rustling Craig Rafter V steers and cows.

For Branch Craig swore that Rafter V was being rustled. He claimed his spread was losing cattle in great numbers. And hadn't Dee Bowden built up his Diamond inside a Diamond herd rather rapidly?

"This don't look good," Dee murmured.

"It sure doesn't," Nancy conjured.

Dee glanced across the dancers. His eyes fell on big Mark Stratton, owner of Round Rock's only saloon, The Diamond Willow. An expensive blue serge suit covered the saloon man's wide shoulders. He judged Stratton to be in his middle thirties.

Stratton had been in Round Rock almost a year now. He had come from nowhere, just stepping down from the stage one summer afternoon. Old Happy Jayson had then owned The Diamond Willow.

Jayson had owned the saloon for years and years. Under his tutelage all had been run honestly, the poker and crap games toeing the lines but with Stratton as Diamond Willow owner—

Stratton had girls upstairs, a point which irritated the

8

town matrons. Stratton had been in Round Rock only a month when Happy Jayson had hanged himself upstairs over The Diamond Willow.

Jayson's actions had amazed the town. Jayson had been a short, pot-bellied man with a wry humor—the last person Round Rock picked to commit suicide. He had left one heir, a nephew back east.

The nephew had come to Round Rock, looked things over, found them not to his liking, and had sold the Diamond Willow to Mark Stratton at a ridiculous low figure, and then had departed for home in Pennsylvania.

Stratton danced with one of his girls, a little blonde thing called Millie. Every time Dee had met Millie on the street—or in The Diamond Willow—Millie had had a nice smile for him.

Usually The Diamond Willow girls just came and went but Millie had been in Round Rock some six months now. Gossip claimed her Mark Stratton's favorite. Stratton had become one of Round Rock's most stalwart citizens.

Evidently Stratton had money. He gave a donation to each and every public cause. Rumor claimed he had invested quite a sum in John Hendrick's bank, the Wyoming National Bank—Round Rock's only bank.

Prior to Hendricks opening the Wyoming National, Round Rock citizens had had to bank in Blasted Stone, a cowtown some thirty miles straight north. Rafter V was eighteen miles due south of Blasted Stone.

Evidently Branch Craig intended to put his cattle-money in Blasted Stone's Community Bank, where he had banked prior to the opening of Wyoming National in Round Rock.

Dee's Beaver Creek Springs' ranch was seven miles straight south of Rafter V, and five miles straight north of Round Rock. His herd was being held on Greasewood Flats two miles northeast of town.

He looked about for lanky John Hendricks. Both Hendricks and Stratton were bachelors, Stratton living in quarters over his Diamond Willow and Hendricks in quarters adjacent to the rear of his bank.

Hendricks was easy to locate. He was so tall he stood out over the dancers, as did Dee Bowden. Hendricks danced with a Diamond Willow girl known only as Vivian.

Vivian was a pretty brunette. A very tight and short dress accentuated her slender waist. She smiled up at Hendrick's. Dee judged Hendricks and Stratton to both be about the same age—in their late thirties or very early forties.

Dee had a sudden comical thought: Where was Banker John Hendricks' rifle? Of course, the banker couldn't dance with a rifle in hand, but Hendricks was never very far from his .25-20 Winchester repeater.

The rifle rested beside him, barrel upward, as he clerked in his bank. He carried it with him on the streets and into public buildings.

Dee had seen Hendricks—and the .25-20—in action. One evening in July Dee had been riding out of Round Rock when Hendricks had been rifle-practicing on the edge of town in the sagebrush close to the town dump.

Dee had pulled in his bronc, watching in amazement. The banker was an expert with the light rifle.

Hendricks could throw up a can and hit it three times before the can crashed to the ground, shooting from the hip. From the shoulder, the banker could hit the can at least five times before the can landed.

Dee held Nancy close, remembering he owed Hendricks four thousand dollars. The past winter had hung on and on, blizzard after blizzard sweeping northwest Wyoming.

Dee had been forced to buy hay. Tomorrow he'd ship out two hundred head of his Diamond inside a Diamond steers and dry cows.

Each beef would bring at least thirty dollars, cash from buyers as the animal was loaded. Thirty times two hundred was six thousand dollars.

He'd pay Hendricks in full. He'd have two thousand left over to see him and his cattle through the oncoming winter.

One of his cowboys—a middle-aged rider named Hank Byers—now held the Diamond inside a Diamond herd on Greasewood Flats. He'd given Byers strict orders under no circumstances to leave the herd alone.

Branch Craig claimed Rafter V was being rustled. Rustlers were known to have in the past stolen entire herds. Dee was taking no chances. Therefore he suddenly stopped dancing when he saw Hank Byers enter the Cowman's Hall's wide doorway.

"What's the matter?" Nancy Craig asked.

"That cowboy— In the doorway— Just entered— He's my hand, Hank Byers."

"I see him. Yes, it's Byers. But what about it?"

"I left him alone watchin' my herd on Greasewood. I gave him orders under no circumstances to abandon the herd. Somethin' must be wrong—"

Dee pushed through the dancers with wild-beating heart, Nancy Craig following. Byers still stood in the doorway looking anxiously left and right. Upon seeing Dee, the cowboy's whiskery face showed relief.

Dee roughly grabbed Byers' skinny shoulder. "What the hell you doin' here, Byers? I told you never to leave the cattle alone!"

"I just had to see you, Dee. Two riders circled the herd an' then rode west into the rimrock. I tried to head them off to talk to them but they always stayed out of range."

"They rode into the rimrock—to the west?"

"Yeah... They built a fire there—a campfire— Close to Chimney Butte. I could see it as I circled the dogies. I swear to the Almighty that they're there for no good."

Dee paused. A high rimrock ridge ran straight north to the Montana border. His Beaver Creek Springs ranch—and Branch Craig's Rafter V—squatted at the foot of this

11

high escarpment's eastern flank.

"How long ago was this, Byers?"

"I saw them make camp. Then headed into town as fast as my cayuse would take me, boss! I just had to ride in—warn you— One man alone with all that responsibiity of that herd—"

Dee dug out his dollar Ingersoll pocket-watch. Ten to nine. The dance was just about an hour old. Darkness came early to this high northern range at this time of the year.

Logic came in. Even if his herd were rustled in this short time rustlers could not have moved the dogies very far. He and Byers would soon catch up. Dee looked about for Shorty Messenger. He'd take Shorty—his only other hand—with them.

Still, something seemed missing. He couldn't lay his thumb on just what made premonitions possess him. Actually, Hank Byers had had no real reason for abandoning the herd, riding into Round Rock.

Apparently the pair of riders had taken no overt action against him or Diamond inside a Diamond cattle. Dee's roving eyes finally located Shorty. Shorty danced with Henrietta Stevens, a very popular local belle.

Henrietta was so popular her dance-card had evidently been filled within a few minutes after she'd entered. Therefore Shorty had waited some time for this dance.

Dee didn't have the heart to take Shorty from Henrietta. He'd go alone with Byers.

Common sense told Dee Bowden that winter was but a month or so away. Ranches laid off cowboys come winter-time. Ranches then cut back on cowhands. The pair seen by Hank Byers could be only transient cowboys heading south to a climate that better fitted their clothes.

And drifters had every right to camp in the rimrock-badlands, for this huge wilderness area was government range—open range. Few cattle ran back in that desolate area for it was a region of short salt grass and very little

12

rain. Only strays and mavericks ventured into that section.

"Did I do right, boss?" Hank Byers asked.

Dee said to Nancy, "Got to ride, Nancy," and then to his cowboy, "You did right, Byers."

"That's a load off my mind," Hank Byers said.

Chapter Two

Dee's buckskin was in the Town Livery Barn. Byers led his bay gelding. Dee noticed the bay did not breathe too hard and surely Byers must have pushed the bronc fast into town.

"Nancy Craig likes you," Byers said.

Dee said, "Her father definitely doesn't."

Byers had no reply. Two weeks back a pitman-rod had broken on one of Dee's movers and he'd ridden to Round Rock to buy a new one. The rod tied behind his saddle, he saw no Rafter V broncs tied in front of Stratton's Diamond Willow—and he decided to go in for a cold beer.

Unbeknown to him, Rafter V had its broncs hitch-racked in the alley. And Branch Craig had stood at the bar in the midst of a dozen Rafter V cowhands—all tough transplanted Texans.

Craig saw Dee in the backbar mirror. "Well, look what the damned wind blew in, men! The local cattle-king, himself!"

Dee stopped just inside the door. It was too late to back out. He wanted no trouble with Nancy's father. And the half-filled whiskey-bottle in front of Craig told him that once more Craig had been drinking heavily.

Branch Craig's narrowed eyes watched Dee closely in the mirror. "He starts out with one single milk cow. Now he owns over a thousan' head of Wyomin' dogies."

The Rafter V cowhands said nothing but Dee noticed they were discreetly moving further to the left and right of their gruff and tough boss.

And Branch Craig had laughed nastily. "Maybe he swings a fast loop? Maybe he rides a fast cayuse? An' maybe that rope he swings is plenty long?"

Anger stormed Dee. A *fast loop* meant you roped the other guy's cattle. A *fast cayuse* meant you rode a fast horse that could take up to that running cow within a few feet.

A *long rope* meant you packed forty or fifty feet of manila while the average waddy had a thirty foot rope. Branch Craig was calling him a cowthief—a rustler—

"You've been drinkin', Craig."

Branch Craig had again laughed. He had turned to face Dee with his gun-harness creaking and his savage-pointed Taos spur-rowels and chains making a disagreeable clinking that cut across the sudden silent tension holding The Diamon Willow. His savage eyes met Dee's angry eyes.

Dee spoke through controlled anger. "I never had no parents. I was dropped off a passin' wagon train when a mere baby. Mrs. Rothwell down at the hotel raised me, God bless her big soul!"

"Amen to that, Bowden."

The solemn words had come from Mark Stratton, who was tending bar. Mrs. Rothwell had died three months ago. Mark Stratton had eaten in the hotel dining room since coming to Round Rock.

"I thank you, sir," Dee told the saloon-keeper. "Mrs. Rothwell was more than a mother to me. She was also a very dear friend."

"Let's not get sentimental," Branch Craig growled, heavy hand resting on his holstered .45's black butt. "We're jus' interested in one thing—How come you have so many cows under your brand in such a short time?"

"I want no trouble with you, Craig."

"I asked a question, remember?"

"Very simple. Mrs. Rothwell bought me my first heifer when I was six. That heifer had a calf. That calf had a calf in time. I sold and bought and traded."

"Now you got around a thousan' head, huh?"

"An' every head honestly come by. I never let my poor cattle winter-kill. I've always scrounged up hay for winter feedin', something you never did—and a few years ago you lost by the thousands to that late Spring storm."

Dee spoke truth. Every manjack in the saloon knew this. When fifteen he had settled on Beaver Creek Springs even though he'd had no legal claim to that area.

Mrs. Rothwell had engineered this plan. She'd argued that possession had been nine points of the law and that when Dee was twenty-one he could legally file a homestead claim on Beaver Creek Springs.

This Dee had done last year. He was now proving-up on the bubbling, ever-flowing Springs. Within a few days Uncle Sam would be sending him his final papers. Beaver Creek Springs would then legally be his homestead property.

During summer dry spells, water was gold here in drouth-stricken Wyoming. Dee's settling on Beaver Creek Springs had not endeared him to big Branch Craig who needed Beaver Creek water for his thousands of longhorns.

Craig, rumor had said, had had his eye also on Beaver Creek Springs, for whoever controlled the Springs controlled all water miles below in Beaver Creek—but Craig had acted too late. Dee Bowden—fifteen, grinning, blonde—had already controlled the Springs.

Dee spoke slowly. "I built windbreaks for my stock at Beaver Creek Springs. My cows stood protected. They didn't need to try to forage on open range with grass frozen down so deep they eventually died."

"You tryin' to tell me how to run cows, Bowden?"

"I'm tellin' you what I did to build up my herd. I've been fifteen years buildin' up my herd. I've never laid a rope on any cow—or calf or bull—other than my own,

16

Craig. You called me a rustler, a cow-thief. There's no lower words in this country. Now back up your words!"

Dee had had enough. In fact, Dee Bowden had had too much.

He thought momentarily of Nancy, down in Cheyenne finishing normal school. He liked Nancy Craig. They'd been friends since childhood. He felt sure Nancy liked him. Anyway, he hoped so.

Dismay tugged his heart. He might kill Nancy's father. Or Nancy's father might kill him.

Dee knew he was no hand as a gunman. And Branch Craig—? Craig had faced a number of fast gunmen with roaring .45s. Craig had proven his gunspeed and accuracy under fire, something Dee definitely had not done.

Rafter V hands had now moved far to either side. Branch Craig stood alone at the bar. Mark Stratton also had moved his blue-serged bulk a safe distance to Craig's left.

Stratton watched through lidded, thoughtful eyes. For some reason, Dee Bowden got the sudden impression that Stratton would welcome gunplay in which he or Craig— or both—were killed.

He pushed that silly idea aside, concentrating on Branch Craig. He had challenged Craig. Would Craig respond? Dee's knuckles were white on his .45's walnut grip.

But evidently Branch Craig had to have his say before pulling. His coarse voice said, "I've run out tallies, Bowden. The last year— I've lost lots of stock. Steers, cows, even suckin' calves. And I cain't forget your brand. A Diamond inside a Diamond."

Dee said, "I know damn' well what's eatin' you, Craig. You think I've been changin' your Rafter V into a Diamond inside a Diamond."

Dee spoke truth. Both he and Craig branded on the right ribs. A man with a hot running-iron could change the Rafter to a big Diamond. Then the smoking iron could run an inverted V over the original V.

In this way, a Rafter V could be changed to a Diamond inside a Diamond, Dee's registered brand.

Dee said, "I never asked for the Diamond inside a Diamond iron, Craig. The Territorial Brandin' Iron Commission jus' told me to bran' with that bran', and I had to do it. I've petitioned for a new an' different bran' but the Commission has said *no*."

There was a short, freighted silence—the ugly silence before roaring, blasting action. Dee had noticed Banker John Hendricks sitting in the corner. The money-man had been talking to blonde Millie, his rifle upright in the corner.

He had had a glimpse of Millie disappearing through the rear door, but had paid it no never mind. Now, without warning, Millie barged in the front door, Sheriff Isaac Watson trailing her, gun out.

The lawman's long mustaches trembled. "What's goin' on in here?" his squeaky voice demanded.

"He's going to kill Dee!" Millie wailed.

Dee hid surprise. He meant nothing to this lovely dance-hall girl. He had never even bought her so much as a beer.

"Dee's too young to die!" Millie added, wiping tears away.

"He won't die," Sheriff Watson said. His pale blue fifty-year-old eyes raked Branch Craig. "This girl tells me you accuse young Dee here of rustlin' Rafter V cattle?"

"That I do."

"You got any proof?"

"One brockle-faced four-year-old cow in his herd sure looks like one that used to wear my iron and run range up in the Larb Hills," the cowman said. "Damn it, he even brands where I do—on the right ribs!"

Sheriff Watson's pale eyes stabbed Dee. Watson had been sheriff longer than most Round Rock citizens could remember. Some claimed him too weak to meet serious trouble if it arose.

During Watson's long tenure, Round Rock County

had had no serious lawlessness. Branch Craig and his gunhung riders and their handy catchropes had seen to that. Rustlers unfortunate enough to even attempt to steal a Rafter V cow did not end up in court.

They ended up as cottonwood bait. Dangling from a cottonwood trees stout branch, boots a few feet off the ground.

"I raised that brockle-faced from a calf," Dee said. "If Mrs. Rothwell was here, she could prove it."

"But she ain't here," Branch Craig snarled, "an' she'll never come back. I'd like to kill that cow. Skin 'er. Scrape from inside. See if there ain't trace of my ol' Rafter V iron inside her hide."

"You can do that any time you want to," Dee said, "but first you pay me for the cow, Craig. I give you nothin', not even time of the day."

"You young whippersnapper—"

Face flushed with rage, Branch Craig started his draw. Moving quickly despite his age, Sheriff Isaac Watson threw himself on the cowman's gunarm, skinny hands savagely clutching Craig's forearm.

"No you don't, Branch! This is foolishness!"

Dee Bowden's gun was half out of leather. He realized that Branch Craig had had him beaten. Craig could have killed him had it not been for Sheriff Watson.

"Oh, heavens," Millie said.

Mark Stratton said nothing. He watched through heavy eyes. Banker John Hendricks has merely braced his chair on its two hind legs, back against the wall. Dee saw him smile. An amused smile? Hendricks' rifle still stood in the corner.

He got the impression suddenly that Hendricks would have been happy to have seen the guns lift, level, roar—and kill. He hastily discarded such a thought. He owed Hendricks money. With him dead—and no heirs to the Diamond within a Diamond—

Logic then came in. With him dead, Hendricks could legally claim Diamond within a Diamond on basis of the debt. Suddenly, Dee Bowden's blood sickened. Sheriff Isaac Watson was correct. This had turned into a travesty!

He turned to leave, gun down now in holster. Branch Craig's rough words halted him at the door.

"I still might have to kill you, Bowden!"

"Maybe I'll kill you first," Dee reminded, and instantly regretted his words as Sheriff Watson had said sternly, "Them's threatenin' words, men. They can be held ag'in you in court!"

Dee had glanced at Millie. "I thank you, lady."

He had left.

Now, hurrying toward the Town Livery Barn, Dee Bowden had a premonition of impending danger hanging over his broad shoulders. He decided to drink no more this night. Alcohol only distorted his judgment, he knew.

Had Branch Craig not been half-drunk two weeks ago, he'd probably not have threatened him. And had he not been so angry, he undoubtedly would not have threatened Branch Craig, either.

A few minutes later, he and Hank Byers loped past the Cowman's Hall and its glaring kerosene lamps, the rest of town except The Diamond Willow being dark—all town occupants except a few drunks being at the Hall.

Big Mark Stratton stood alone in front of the Hall, the overhead lantern reflecting from his blue serge suit. He lifted a hand idly as Dee Bowden and Byers loped by.

Dee wondered why the saloon-man had been in front of the Hall. And alone, too. Had Stratton come out to see which way he and Byers were going? That thought was foolish. What he did—where he went— Well, Stratton was not concerned with his procedures.

The two loped into a star-filled Wyoming night. There was no moon but brilliant starlight outlined sagebrush, greasewood, *arroyos* and tall buttes standing magnificently with scraggly mesas beyond them.

Then, the rimrock came in to the west. A flat, igneous high ledge, it ran for miles and miles north and south, marking the western edge of huge Round Rock Basin.

The fall wind was chilly coming down from the distant snow-tipped Teton Mountains where lately the discovery of gold had caused a gold-rush, Dee had heard. Soon winter would be here. Dee was prepared. He and his two hands had cut much native bluejoint hay on the prairie and had stacked it for winter feeding.

They'd repaired snowsheds and snowfences for cattle to stand behind and have windbreaks against blizzards.

Dee glanced at Byers who rode high in leather, bony body angled against the chilly wind—and again Dee Bowden realized he knew little, if anything, about this cowboy.

Byers had drifted in ten months ago asking for a job. He'd proven a good worker and he'd also proven tight-lipped. Dee had no idea where Byers had come from before riding into Dee's Beaver Creek Springs camp.

Although he and Byers had pitched hay shoulder-to-shoulder, Byers had not mentioned a word of his past.

Dee also rode high on oxbow stirrups, peering into the starlight for the first glimpse of his herd, his mind on Branch Craig and Craig's allegations that Rafter V was losing stock to rustlers.

Dee realized Branch Craig was telling the truth. Craig knew his range and knew his cattle even though they numbered in thousands. Craig was, above all, a cowman—bred and born to the saddle and lass-rope. And when Craig said he lost cattle, Craig lost cattle.

Dee knew that Craig had a number of head of cattle he used as markers—cattle marked by accidents or nature to be easily recognizable. A horn knocked down. A hide marked by a specific natural design like a white area against black. A steer with a bum hip.

Craig said he'd even lost a few markers. Where were his cattle going? It was one thing to rustle and another to dispose of the cows you'd rustled, Dee knew. Sudden relief flooded him. He saw his herd ahead in the starlight.

Most of the Wyoming dogies were bedded down,

backs to the wind. Only a few grazed. They lifted their heads and studied the two riders. They then continued grazing the short fall grass.

"Circle opposite," Dee ordered.

Byers rode into the night around the cattle, singing softly. Dee rode the other direction. They met on the opposite side of the heard. "All okay," Dee said. "Markers are there."

"Guess I spread a false alarm, Boss."

Dee slouched in leather. "Be happy when these bossies are all in cattle-cars tomorrow headin' east."

Because he was Round Rock's biggest rancher, Branch Craig had been given the honor of shipping the first cattle over the newly-laid rails. Now Dee remembered that Rafter V had shipped some seventy odd cattle-cars east that afternoon, a small fortune in livestock.

Dee swung in saddle, hands braced on fork and pommel, and looked at the rimrock. "No fires there," he said.

"Drifters prob'ly rode on."

Dee straightened. "I'll send Shorty out when I get back in town. Under no circumstances leave this herd alone again tonight, understand."

"I'm damn' sorry, boss. But—"

Dee glanced at the Northern Star. "Mite after ten. I'll be out around one. Where abouts did you see that campfire?"

Byers pointed toward the western rimrock. "Right about where Chimney Butte is, boss. Mite to the left."

"I'll ride over there and look around."

Want me to go with you? They might be holed up—"

"I'll make it alone."

"Want me to ride with you, boss?"

"Those riders were evidently drifters. They'll be miles away by now. Or sleepin' in their bedrolls." Dee looked toward the western rimrock. A dark high igneous ledge, black and ominous under starlight, it stretched north and south, a barrier erected by fickle nature. "Thanks, though."

Byers turned his bronc east. I'll circle and sing to 'em." He disappeared in the Wyoming starlight.

Dee turned Sonny straight west. He knew the rimrock well. The rock barrier was broken in a few places as trails wound up these canyons to the high mesa and badlands beyond.

Chimney Butte reared its awesome heights. He rode toward it. Within ten minutes he crossed the wide wagon road leading north to his Diamond in a Diamond and the huge Branch Craig iron's buildings sprawled out along Sagebrush Creek, some nine miles north.

This was the trail Branch Craig—and his big supply of money—had taken after leaving Round Rock. Dee looked south. Starlight was bright but he could not see the log cabin of old Wolf Nelson, the trapper, a mile south on the road.

Wolf Nelson was an ancient who had come into this area before the Civil War—one of the original buckskin men. He trapped—and poisoned—wolves and coyotes for the Territorial government, which paid him a bounty for each set of wild canine ears he turned in to Sheriff Isaac Watson.

Rumor had it that Wolf had worn out squaw after squaw as wives. Dee remembered Wolf's last squaw—a fat, slow-walking Shoshoni. Wolf now lived alone. He was drunk most of the time.

He made his own whiskey back in the brush along Wilderness Creek. He raised a bit of wheat and corn each year, the only work he did outside of riding out wintertime to check his traps.

Dee was against trapping canine predators. He had yet to find a carcass of a calf killed by a wolf or coyote. He admitted each sometimes killed lambs but there were no sheep on Round Rock range.

For each wild canine killed, dozens of jackrabbits were insured life to eat precious grass needed for his cattle and the steers and cows of other Round Rock ranchers.

Wolf Nelson had evidently heard of Dee's stand on Wolf's trapping, for he had in Round Rock a year ago told Dee to mind his own business and keep his mouth shut.

Dee crossed the wagon-trail, wondering why he spent so much time thinking of miserable old Wolf Nelson. Had Wolf been a young man, he and Dee Bowden would have tangled with guns or fists, then and there.

But Dee had just walked away from the drunk.

Wagon-trail behind, Dee rode upslope toward the rimrock, which grew darker and more overpowering as he neared. He found the canyon threading westward along the south base of Chimney Butte.

He rode up it a mile, Sonny sweating as he climbed. Finally Dee and his buckskin topped a small mesa.

Dee saw no fire burning ahead. He decided to return to Cowman's Hall. Byers had imagined things. He neck-reined Sonny around, pointing the buckskin east. Then, suddenly, he pulled up short, the buckskin standing still, breathing deeply, ribs rising and falling under the saddle cinch.

He had heard a shot. Sounded like a distant rifle shot. Or had he been wrong? Was he, too, imagining things?

While turning, Sonny's off-hoof had clanged its steel shoe against a boulder. Maybe that was what he had heard? No, it had been a shot.

Dee Bowden pushed back his new Tom Watson Stetson and scratched his head, deciding he'd not heard a shot. He touched his Kelly spurs to Sonny, who moved on down-slope.

Once free of the canyon, Dee pointed his bronc southeast, cutting across country toward Round Rock, some three miles away. He did not follow the wagon trail until he hit it a few rods north of the cowtown.

Wolf Nelson's cabin lay to his left. He saw its outlines some quarter mile away. It had no lights.

When he rode past Cowman's Hall banker John Hendricks had just left the building carrying his rifle, apparently heading home. The banker stopped and said, "Night ride, Bowden?"

"Night ride."

"Your horse breathes hard. Been runnin', huh?"

Dee had irritation. His actions were not accountable to this banker. He said gruffly, "Tomorrow I pay you in cash completely after I'm paid for my stock," and rode on toward the livery-barn.

When dismounting in front of the barn, he glanced back. Hendricks was not in sight. He'd not had time to walk to the bank. Dee judged the man had returned to the dance.

He looked about for the barn's owner, middle-aged Jake Spooner. Spooner was not hard to find. He slept drunkedly in a manger.

Dee did not unsaddle. He merely unloosened his cinch after watering Sonny at the trough. He'd have a dance or so—preferably with Nancy—and then head out to his herd, taking Shorty Messenger along.

The dance was in full swing. Again fiddles squeaked, the accordion wheezed. A group of cowboys stood in front passing a bottle around. "Have a snort, Dee."

"No, thanks, Tony."

"Dee, not drinkin'— Sick, Dee?"

Dee had known Tony Matthews all his life. "Mortally wounded, Tony." He entered the Hall.

Hendricks danced with Vivian, the Diamond Willow girl. Hendrick's rifle leaned against the wall close to the bass-fiddle player.

Shorty Messenger again danced with Henrietta Stevens. Shorty was doing all right. Dee looked for Nancy Craig.

Nancy danced with a Rafter V cowboy.

Dee saw that little blonde Millie, the other Diamond Willow girl, sat alone on a long bench. Millie and Vivian always sat alone at a dance for no town matron or miss would disgrace herself by sitting next to a saloon-girl.

Dee went to Millie. "This dance, please, Miss Millie."

"With pleasure."

Millie fitted nicely into his arms. She was curves and

cuddly. Dee swung her out on the floor. His glance clased with that of Nancy. Nancy scowled. Nancy apparently didn't like his dancing with a saloon-girl?

Dee hid his grin.

"Thanks for bringing Sheriff Watson the other day," Dee said.

"I thought it best, Dee."

"I'm no gunhand. Craig could've killed me. You saved my life."

Millie then looked up momentarily, then dropped her eyes. Dee was surprised to see tears in her blue eyes. "It was nothing, Dee."

Dee wondered why she cried, but his bewilderment did not last long. A loud voice from the doorway called, "Sheriff Watson!"

The voice cut across the music. The music stopped. The dancers stopped. A skinny old cowboy stood in the doorway. He stood on tiptoe looking for the sheriff who called back, "Over here, Jepperson. What'd you want?"

The sheriff pushed through the crowd, mustaches twitching. He'd been dancing with his obese wife, mother of his twelve children. Dee said, "Excuse me," and also pushed toward Jepperson.

Smoky Jepperson's leather face was red from the raw wind and his excitement.

"Sheriff, Branch Craig—"

"What about Craig?" Sheriff Watson demanded.

"I was ridin' into town— Found him beyond Wolf Nelson's shack— He's layin' on the wagon-trail— He's—"

"He's what, Jepperson?"

"He's dead!"

"Dead?"

"Murdered, sheriff!"

"Murdered?"

"Shot in the back, sheriff!"

Chapter Three

Dee heard Nancy Craig cry out in stricken grief. He turned and looked back at her, one thought driving through his memory.

Devil's Canyon. His thinking he heard a rifle shot straight east down on the level country.

Mr. and Mrs. Swanson were assisting Nancy toward a bench. Dee's attention returned to Smoky Jepperson.

"How'd you know he was shot in the back?" Sheriff Watson asked.

"He lays face down— I lit a match. Bullet hole in his back, just behin' his heart— I turned him over. Bigger bullet hole in the front where the lead came out."

"Soft nosed slug," the sheriff said. "Expanded as it hit flesh. You check his pockets?"

"No."

"His horse?"

"Stood uptrail a hundred feet or so, reins ground-tyin' him."

"You check the saddle-bags?"

"No."

Sheriff Watson tugged his mustaches, face graven. "He's been ambushed an' robbed. He'll have no money on him or in his bags. Mack, run get Doc Estambres."

"Okay, sheriff."

The townsman scurried away. Doc Estambres had come to Round Rock a few years before. He claimed to have a college degree as a veterinarian, a point many doubted.

He also served as doctor to humans in addition to compounding medicines in his drugstore. Dee judged the pseudo doctor to be close to seventy. Because of his age, he evidently had not attended the dance.

"Wonder who shot him? Branch sure never had many enemies." The words came from Saloonman Mark Stratton, who had moved in on Dee's right.

The word *enemies* had turned all eyes on Dee Bowden. For the first time, Dee realized his predicament.

"You rode out a while back, didn't you, Bowden?" Sheriff Isaac Watson's voice was suddenly hard and cold.

"My hand, Byers, came in for me. He'd been out with my herd on Greasewood Flats. Saw two riders drift past about sundown. They rode up Devil Canyon toward Chimney Butte."

"Yeah. . . . Go on, please."

All eyes were on Dee. Dee glanced at Nancy, not sitting on a bench. Nancy's eyes met his. Dee was the one who looked away. He remembered the Diamond Willow and two cowmen—one middle-aged, the other young—going for their guns.

"Byers waited a while, got scared, came in for me. I rode out to my herd. Nothing wrong there. I trailed up Devil a ways, got to Chimney, saw nothing suspicious— no drifters—"

"An' then you returned here?"

"Yes."

"Here comes Doc," a man said.

Sheriff Isaac Watson nodded. "He can be explained to on the ride out to Branch's body. Bowden, you ride with us, savvy?"

Dee was aware that banker John Hendricks, rifle in hand, had moved in on his left, penning him between himself and heavy-set, tough Mark Stratton. "I'll gladly ride, sheriff."

Within minutes, the group thundered out of Round Rock, the dance forgotten and finished.

28

Sheriff Watson and Dee headed the hard-riders. Behind them and spread out on either side thundered Mark Stratton and John Hendricks, about fifty curious townsmen riding behind the saloonman and banker.

Sheriff Watson reined his plunging black gelding close. "Why'd Byers ride in for you, Bowden?"

Dee told him.

The lawman settled back in saddle. "Byers always has looked like a tough nut to me, Bowden—one who doesn't dodge trouble. What you tol' me sure doesn't sound like Byers to me!"

Dee silently agreed.

Dust rising in starlight, they galloped past Wolf Nelson's one room log cabin, his hounds barking wildly in their enclosure. The cabin was dark and no kerosene lamp was lighted although Dee was sure the group made enough hoof-noise to awaken the dead.

Nelson was probably sleeping dead-drunk.

They came to the body a short distance below the point where Dee had ridden across the wagon-trail heading for Devil's Canyon. They pulled in and dismounted with Sheriff Isaac Watson saying, "Dee, put your back to me. I want your pistol."

Dee turned. He felt his .45 leave his flank.

"He's got a rifle in his saddle-boot," a townsman said.

Watson spoke to Mark Stratton. "Pull his rifle. Smell it. Hs it been fired lately?"

Stratton smelled. "He could have cleaned it. He's got a cleanin' rod in the saddle-boot."

"Let me smell the barrel," Hendricks said.

Somebody came in with a lighted lantern. As Smoky Jepperson had said, Branch Craig lay on his back. Sheriff Watson went to one knee beside the corpse of his long-time friend.

Doc Estambres got to his knees with difficulty on Craig's other side. All watched as the pseudo doctor checked the cowman's pulse. Doc Estambres said, "He's dead as he ever will be."

Banker Hendrick's said, "This rifle could have been

recently fired, then cleaned."

"Stratton said the same," Dee Bowden said shortly.

Sheriff Watson finished searching the body. He opened Branch Craig's wallet. Except for a few coins, it held no bills.

"Branch always carried a coupla hundred in foldin' money," the sheriff said.

"Robbed," a man said.

Another man said, "He got paid a heck of a lot of money. Too much for a wallet to carry. Here comes Harper with Branch's hoss."

Sheriff Watson got to his feet. "Keep Bowden's rifle," he said to Hendricks." He searched the saddlebags. "Fence pliers. Some tools, but not a damned bit of currency."

"Killed for his money," a man uselessly said.

Dee Bowden's future looked bleak, and Dee Bowden would have been the first to so admit. He realized even Hank Byers' testimony could not help him. Rather, it would be damaging.

For Byers would testify that he had seen his boss ride west toward the black maw of Devil's Canyon. And all would then know that Dee had crossed this wagon-trail around this point of murder.

Dee glanced at Sonny. A townsman held his buckskin by the reins. He'd had a sudden, wild plan that called for his launching himself on his horse and spurring the fast bronc into the starlight.

Now that plan—stupid as it had been—was gone.

"What'll we do with the body?" Mark Stratton asked.

Sheriff Watson rubbed his hands together. "Weather's gettin' cold. Goin' be a hard winter, the Sioux say. Smith's comin' out with his funeral wagon to pick up Branch."

There was a moment of silence. Dee noticed some had doffed hats to hold them over their hearts. His anger against his hypocrisy grew. Branch Craig had been domineering and arrogant. He felt sure almost every man-jack here had been angry at Branch sometime in his life. Now all wept crocodile tears.

Sheriff Watson said, "Come on, Bowden. We ride out to your herd an' talk to Hank Byers."

"He'll tell you the same thing I've told you."

"That may be, but we'll get it from a different angle, maybe."

"He should be handcuffed, sheriff," a man said.

Dee looked at the speaker—a squat broad-shoulder man of his age. He and Luther MacCready had been enemies since first-grade days. They had fought many times, most fistfights ending in a draw. They just seemed to instinctively dislike the other.

"You the law here, Luther?" Dee Bowden's voice held cynicism.

"No, I ain't the law, Bowden. If I was, you'd be in irons with the evidence everybody's got ag'in you, you bushwhackin' son!"

Fists knotted, Dee started for MacCready, who readily stepped forward, fists also knotted. Townsmen crowded between them with Sheriff Isaac Watson saying angrily, "None of that, you two!"

Dee Bowden stopped struggling. Wasting time—and strength—on MacCready would be a complete waste. And he might only earn another black eye.

"Tie his hands behin' him," MacCready said.

Sheriff Watson said, "You ain't my deputy, Mac-Cready. Mount your cayuse, Bowden. Wilson, hang onto the buckskin's reins. Lead his hoss."

"Okay, sheriff."

Watson spoke to Dee, now mounted. "Lead us to your herd, Bowden."

The mounted group left the wagon-trail. One man stayed behind—Smoky Jepperson—to guard the body. The horses were pointed northeast toward Greasewood Flats, Wilson and Sheriff Watson taking the lead, Wilson leading Sonny with Dee Bowden sitting helplessly in saddle.

"Come up easy on my dogies," Dee warned. "I don't want no stampede to run the fat off'm them cattle."

"I'll see they don't get runnin', boss."

31

The words came from Shorty Messenger. Dee had been so busy he'd not noticed his other cowhand in the group.

"I'll ride ahead," Shorty said, "an' tell Byers who we are."

"Good idea," Sheriff Watson said.

Shorty touched spurs to his pinto and loped ahead into the starlight. Within a mile, the squat cowpuncher was seen returning, dust behind him in the starlight, another rider pounding at his horse's hoofs. The two drew rein around Dee and the sheriff.

"What t'hell happened, boss?" Byers asked.

Dee said, "The sheriff will tell you." He sat saddle and listened. Yes, he'd ridden into town for Dee. Yes, there'd been two suspicious riders. Yes, Dee had ridden west toward Chimney Butte.

"Did you hear any rifle shootin' after Dee left?" Sheriff Watson asked.

The lawman shot the question across the chilly Wyoming air. For a long second silence held the riders. All eyes were on the homely face of Hank Byers.

Byers seemed reluctant to answer.

"What's the answer, Byers?" the sheriff growled.

Byers looked at Dee. "I have to tell the truth, boss." Then, to Sheriff Isaac Watson, "Yes, I did hear a rifle report."

"How many?" Watson demanded.

"Jus' one shot. Sounded like a .30-30."

Dee's knuckles became white on the saddle's fork. Byers had had no reason for adding that .30-30 business. Byers knew full well he, Dee Bowden, packed a Winchester .30-30 rifle.

But so did almost all the other local cowhands, too. A Winchester .30-30 was a good saddle-gun.

"What direction did this one shot come from?" the sheriff asked.

"Straight west of here."

"The direction Bowden had jus' rid?"

Byers nodded. "That direction. I wondered who was shootin' what at that time of the night. I—"

"No more questions." Sheriff Watson turned on stirrups, staring at Dee. "What plans do you want to make?"

"Plans?"

"Yes, plans."

Dee then understood. He was under arrest, charged with murder—bushwhack, back-shooting murder. He thought of Nancy Craig. He and Nancy— Well, all that was gone now.

He spoke to Shorty Messenger. "You're the boss here until I get back. Byers, be sure you and Shorty have these cattle in the new railroad corrals at the right time—one sharp today noon."

"They'll be there," Byers said and added, "At one, boss."

Dee spoke to Sheriff Isaac Watson. "Let's ride, sheriff."

The riders thundered back towards Round Rock. Dee Bowden looked up at the stars. He might not see them again for a long time...if ever. You can't see stars through a jail-cell's roof.

Or hanging broken-necked from a cottonwood's limb, either.

Chapter Four

Next morning at ten Nancy Craig gripped bars and said, "I wouldn't believe it of you, Dee Bowden, but all circumstances—"

Dee studied her. He was unshaven, he needed a bath, and his right eye glistened in black splendor. "Why did you come here?"

"I— Well, I just had to see you."

"Why?"

"I've known you all my life, Dee, and—" Her hands dropped. She said, "Dee, did you really murder— bushwhack—my father?"

"What do you think?"

"I— I really don't know."

Dee sat on his cell's cot. He'd had a few hours sleep, nothing more. The cot consisted of a concrete ledge protruding from the rock wall. It had no mattress. It sported a single blanket. Toward morning it had grown cold and Dee had done some shivering under the meager cover.

He'd had enough. No, he corrected—he'd had *too much*. He'd been hoping Nancy would not come to visit him in jail. But here she was—big as life—and just as beautiful as ever—

"I did not murder your father, Nancy."

"How can I tell you're not—"

"Lying," Dee finished sourly. "All right, your father was robbed. Okay, they say I robbed him. If I robbed him, where is the money I stole from him?"

"You could have buried it. Somewhere in Devil's Canyon."

Dee got to his feet. He paced two paces south, two north, turned, paced two south—the length of his cell. The county jail was behind the court-house. The old court-house was made of logs but the jail of solid stone with walls three feet thick.

It held but two cells. The other cell was empty.

Dee Bowden stopped. He rolled his blue eyes skyward. "Lord, help me," he said, and meant it. His eyes went back to Nancy. "I carried a shovel with me, huh? Tied across the back of my saddle? Will you do me a favor?"

"What is it?"

"Go home."

Nancy's dark eyes blazed. "You can go to and stay there!" She wheeled on the high heels of her Justin boots and stalked toward old Art Finnegan, the jailer, who stood at the heavy oak door.

Old Art opened the door with his big key. His anger spent, Dee Bowden gripped the bars and watched Nancy's pretty back disappear—and it was indeed a very lovely back, he told himself as he momentarily forgot his dangerous predicament.

"Another female outside to see you, Bowden," old Art wheezed in his asthmatic voice. "Got two ears and a nose, she has."

"You're comical," Dee said. "Send her in."

To his surprise, blonde Millie entered. Dee leaned against the bars and wondered just what was what. "How are you this morning, Dee?"

"Fine. Jus' had my mornin' tea an' crullers, whatever crullers are. How are you?"

"Fine." Millie hesitated, blue eyes sweeping his face. "Your eye— It's blacker'n ever. It fairly glistens."

Dee grinned. "I need a shave, too, but ol' Art won't bring in hot water an' soap an' a razor."

Millie turned and smiled on old Art. "You'll bring

those shaving things now, won't you?"

"For you, but not for him."

Dee understood. The old man had ridden for Branch Craig for years until a bronc had stomped him a few years back. Branch had got him this soft job of county jailer for a jail that nine-tenths of the time was without prisoners.

"Millie don't shave," Doc pointed out.

The old jailer spat. "You know damn' well what I mean, Bowden. I hope to heaven they stretch your neck."

"They do that," Dee said, "an' think of the tax money the county wouldn't get from me—an' you might lose your easy job, old timer."

Millie said, "Have you got a lawyer?"

"Shorty Messenger rode north a few hours ago for Blasted Stone. There's a new young lawyer there named Dave Rutherman. Just graduated from some law school somewhere, Shorty heard."

"How are you going to plead?"

Dee studied her lovely young face. What was amiss here? She was a saloon girl. Some called her a fallen woman, whatever that was. She drank hard liquor, gambled, then plied her ancient trade in the cribs upstairs over the Diamond Willow.

Dee corrected himself on the latter. He'd never seen her in bed with a man. That had been a blow below the belt. But some claimed she was Mark Stratton's woman. Had Stratton sent her over to euchre information out of him?

Dee didn't trust Stratton. The man was too unctious, too oily. The same held for banker John Hendricks and his Winchester .25-20.

Dee realized such mistrust was not just. It was based upon the mistrust an outdoor man—a cowman—has for an indoor man such as a saloon-owner or banker.

"I'll plead the way Lawyer Rutherman tells me," Dee said, thus evading her question.

She nodded gravely. "That's fair enough for an answer. Actually, I realize now I had no right to ask such a silly

36

question. I know you didn't murder Branch Craig."

"I'm glad one woman has faith in me," Dee said. "One just left who apparently had none."

"I waited outside until she had come out. She looked— well, anything but happy. She was crying."

"Cryin'?"

"I guess she likes you."

Dee breathed deeply. "My preliminary hearin' is set for one this afternoon. My attorney should be here by then. If he isn't, I'm goin' ask to have the time set up."

"You have the right to be represented by an attorney."

Dee looked at her. "How did you know that?"

She shrugged, "Maybe I've been arrested a few times?" She laughed a bit too shrilly. She spoke with an eastern accent, Dee had long ago noticed. Undoubtedly she'd been arrested a few times because of her trade? Dee's stomach had a sourness.

"Vistin' time's up," old Art Finnegan said shortly.

Millie said, "Oh, I forgot my basket outside. I've something for you to eat, Dee."

"Good," Dee said. "So far the county has fed me one rotten egg, hardboiled as old Art's head, and two slices of moldy bread. Hope you have a cake with lots of hacksaw blades in it."

"I got to inspect all he eats," old Art pointed out.

Millie hurried out the door, Dee noticing that she also had a very pretty back. She returned with a wicker basket. She handed it to old Art Finnegan who removed the white cloth cover to inspect the basket's contents.

Millie smiled, threw Dee a kiss, and hurried out, this time for good. Dee frowned over the kiss-throwing. Things were piling up fast—too fast. "That's not for you, you ol' goat," he told old Art.

"Guess it's all food," the ancient jailer grumbled. "I'll slide it in to you through the door panel piece by piece cause the basket is too big to be pushed through a hole that small."

37

"Jus' so I get it."

Dee realized that the visits of the two pretty girls had taken his mind off the subject of being hanged for a crime he did not commit. His mind then returned to a subject that had tormented him all the time he'd been in this cell: who had murdered Branch Craig?

The *who* was a mystery. The *why*, there for all the world to see. Craig had carried over forty thousand dollars on him.

Dee sat on the concrete cot munching a doughnut. Had Hank Byers deliberately got him out of town and had him ride into Devil's Canyon so he could come behind and kill Craig without getting the blame—but getting Craig's money?

Dee remembered the feeling of something amiss when Byers had called him from the Cowman's Hall last night, but hunches didn't count. What counted was concrete proof.

There was also this question: Where had Branch Craig been during the time he'd left town until murdered? In that two hours or so he could have ridden the entire twelve miles to his Rafter V ranch, not a few miles out of Round Rock.

This information came out during the coroner's inquest, for young lawyer Dave Rutherman checked in to interview his client at twelve. Dee liked the aggressive young redhead.

Six townsmen sat as coroner's jury. Dee knew each one and each one had known Branch Craig, and all were around Craig's age—a fact Rutherman pointed out to the county attorney, fat middle-aged Wadsworth Emerson.

Emerson merely shrugged. "You'll have to go out of Wyoming Territory if you want jurymen who didn't know Branch. Branch was even territorial representative from this district. There'll be no change of venue on account of the jury, attorney."

"Amen to that," intoned gaunt Olaf Hanson, coroner and justice of the peace. Hanson also owned the only local store, the Merc. He had owned and operated the stage line in and out of Round Rock until yesterday when the railroad's coming had put his stages out of business.

The railroad had brought in a telegraph line. Now Round Rock was connected in more than one way with the outside world. The telegraph line had brought in a handful of newspaper reporters from Cheyenne and Larimee and other points as far south as Denver.

Preliminaries dispensed with, witnesses testified. One was old Wolf Nelson who, when he walked past Dee Bowden to get on the stand, cast an odor of skunk-grease and coyote pelts.

Old Wolf testified that Branch Craig had spent over an hour drinking with him in his log cabin. "Rode in plumb drunk, people. Almost fallin' from his pony. Had I knowed he had thet much money on him I'd not allowed him to ride on. He was my friend."

Old Wolf rubbed dirty knuckles into tear-filled eyes. Attorney Dave Rutherman objected to old Wolf's testimony. "This witness is plainly dead drunk, Your Honor."

J.P. Hanson rapped his bench with his gavel. "You'd never find him sober so his testimony has to stand. Objection over-ruled."

Finally, the jury filed out. Attorney Rutherman cursed under his breath. The jury returned in eight minutes. Dee Bowden should be held for the murder of one Branch Craig.

The jury's foreman commissioned Sheriff Isaac Watson to issue an arrest warrant for said Dee Bowden. The charge: first degree murder.

Attorney Dave Rutherman leaped to his feet. He pointed out that a coroner's jury had no right to render a criminal warrant. J. P. Hanson informed the young lawyer the coroner's jury also sat as a grand jury.

"Where did you learn your law, attorney?"

Rutherman named a hightoned Eastern college.

"Law is a bit different here in Wyoming, attorney. Court is adjourned."

Reporters crowded around Dee and he and Rutherman left. "Give them not a word," Rutherman told his client.

One red-headed reporter pestered Dee by following him. Dee turned, feinted; the reporter went into a crouch. Dee knocked him flat with a right hook.

"I'm going to sue you!"

"Sue and be damned," Dee gritted. "I couldn't be in a worse deal than I am now. A suit will be nothing."

"You're handy with your dukes," Rutherman said.

Dee grinned. "I'll get handier if I ever get out. I take it first degree murder is a non-bailable offense?"

"That it is. I'm going into conference with that bastardly Hanson to try to get it reduced to manslaughter. There isn't enough evidence to substantiate a first degree murder charge.

"I wish you luck."

Rutherman sent him a glance. "You don't seem optimistic."

"I'm not. I know Hanson. He and Branch Craig were old drinkin' pals. They played penny-ante together hour after hour for a hell of a lot of years."

"Damnit, Dee, why didn't you shoot a common stiff, not a territorial representative?"

"I shot nobody," Dee repeated.

Rutherman said, "I'm an attorney, not a detective." They stopped before Dee's cell, Sheriff Isaac Watson and old Art Finnegan trailing.

Finnegan opened the cell door. Dee stepped inside. Sheriff Watson turned and left, bootheels making hollow sounds on concrete.

"I'll report back," Rutherman said. "Soon, I hope. And with good news."

Dee merely nodded. Finnegan snapped shut the door, shook it to test it, then followed the lawyer out, leaving Dee alone.

Dee looked at his dollar watch. Two o'clock, and time his cattle were being loaded. By standing on the edge of the concrete cot he could just look out the corner of the high and small and barred window.

But he could not see the loading yards. All he could see down the alley was the front door of John Hendricks' bank. Disgusted, he sat on the cot, head in hands, trying to think.

He looked up. Attorney Dave Rutherman had entered. "No deal," the attorney said shortly. "That wool-blind old bastard of a Hanson."

"Branch Craig's best friend, remember?"

"I'll think of something, Dee."

"You'll do more than I can do, then."

Rutherman left. Dee heard the switch engine wheeze steam as it shifted cattle cars. He decided to dehorn all his cattle henceforth. Because of their long horns his cattle could be loaded only some fifteen or so to a cattle-car.

With horns cut off, twenty-five head at least could be pushed into one car. The cost of shipping would be cut down much per cow. He heard boots approaching.

Shorty Messenger soon stood before Dee's cell. "We loaded 'em, Dee, and they're headin' for Chicago soon, an' Sheriff Watson collected your money. Here's the receipt from the cow-buyer."

Dee read: $6,245.25. Two-hundred and forty-five dollars and twenty-five cents more than he'd figured, but no elation hit him. Yesterday this time he'd been tickled pink to know the sum was over six thousand but today—

"Sheriff says he'll pay Hendricks that four thousand, if you want him to—and deposit the rest in your name in Hendricks' bank."

Dee laughed sardonically. "You heard what the coroner's jury turned in, didn't you?"

"I did. The whole country is talkin' about it."

"For? Or against?"

Shorty Messenger's loyal young face showed perplexity. "Dee, I hate to tell you this, but it's the truth. There's even talk of a jail-delivery and— Well, you know."

"I know. I suspected this."

Old Art Finnegan had been listening carefully. "You ain't got no call to alarm my prisoner with rumors, Messenger."

Shorty Messenger grabbed the oldster by the scruff. He pushed the protesting jailer out the door and closed it, leaving him and his boss alone.

Old Finnegan hammered the door. "I'll get the sheriff!"

"Go get him," Messenger said. "I'm willin' to go to jail. You got an extra cell, I notice—an' it's empty."

The hammering stopped. Boots scurried toward the court-house. Shorty looked up at the high but barred window.

"My toughest cayuse— A chain— A good ropin' horse—an' a chain—could pull them bars out by the roots, boss."

"Yeah, they could—and you'd be shot from saddle, more'n likely."

"This lynch talk, Dee. It ain't good."

Dee rubbed a whiskery jaw. "Let's wait a while, Shorty. We'll see what Rutherman can do."

"He cain't do nothin'. This country is all for Craig an' ag'in you. People that even hated Craig are now his friends. Accordin' to them, that is—'cause Branch Craig is dead."

"We'll wait a while, Shorty. You're boss of Diamond inside a Diamond. Where's Byers?"

"He helped load the dogies, then went to the Diamond Willow. You ever notice that Byers an' this Stratton are purty good friends?"

"I've noticed."

"What the hell would Stratton—him all dressed up an' with money— Why would he want a bum for a friend?"

"Maybe we read somethin' into it that ain't there?"

"Here comes the sheriff an' Old Art."

Old Art said, "He grabbed me, sheriff. By the neck, he did! An' he threw me outa my own jail."

Dee grinned. "You can throw me out any time you want to, sheriff."

Sheriff Isaac Watson mopped his forehad with a red bandana. "Damn it, Dee, I've got too many troubles, as it is, to ride nurse-maid on your people. Shorty, you'll have to git out!"

"Thet an order, sheriff?"

"An order, Shorty."

Shorty bowed elaborately to Old Art, then to Sheriff Watson. He winked at Dee. "Hang on, *compadre*."

Dee grinned. "What else is there to do?"

Shorty left.

The evening chill of high-country autumn crept into the cell. Dee lay on his concrete bed, thinking. He could come to no other conclusion: Hank Byers had ambushed—and killed—Branch Craig.

Byers had worked it slick. He had lured him, Dee Bowden, out of Round Rock in front of almost everybody in town. There had been no drifters. Dee had ridden west, Byers behind him. Byers had fired that distant rifle-report he'd heard.

Sheer fatigue put Dee into troubled sleep. Red dreams plagued him. He was on Sonny, hands tied behind, the hangman's noose properly fixed to break his neck when the buckskin was led ahead.

Strangely, Branch Craig was alive. Craig would lead Sonny ahead. Craig snarled, "No, you never kilt me, Bowden! But, jes' the same, I'll have the pleasure of killin' you, you cowthief!"

Craig laughed sardonically. He had Sonny's reins tied hard-and-fast around his own saddle-horn. Craig spurred his horse ahead. He fairly jerked the buckskin out from under Dee.

Dee felt his saddle leave beneath him. His boots slipped out of stirrup. He started to fall—

He awakened, stared about. Sanity came. He was in Round Rock's jail. It had all been a dream. A terrible, savage dream—

Merciful sleep returned. This time, no red dreams. Dawn was bitterly cold, reminding him that winter was not far away. Soon this high-altitude Wyoming country would see its first winter-snow.

Old Art Finnegan brought him his breakfast—two eggs fried to brick-hard finish, a cup of cold coffee and two chunks of biscuit apparently toasted. Dee was hungry. He ate rapidly of the poor fare. "You hear about your hired han', that Byers gent?" old Art asked.

"What about Byers?"

"Byers has been murdered!"

Dee Bowden stared upward, mouth agape. "Did I hear you rightly, ol' timer? Hank Byers— He's been killed."

"He's plumb dead, Bowden!"

Chapter Five

Little Millie was leaving just as Shorty Messenger arrived at ten that same morning. Shorty looked back at Millie as she went out the door. He shook his head and said, "Oh, boy!"

Dee sat on the concrete bunk eating his second breakfast and Millie's breakfast beat the first all hollow. "I don't know why," he said.

"Maybe she likes you?"

"Saloon, Shorty. Stratton. Bunks upstairs."

Shorty grinned. "You forget somethin', Dee. Some of those saloon-girls have been mothers of territorial governors an' such big mucky-mucks. You hear about Byers?"

"I've heard, but maybe you got more detail."

Byers had stayed in Round Rock yesterday and Shorty had ridden home to Diamond inside a Diamond. "This mornin' I noticed Byers hadn't come in durin' the night. Ol' Wolf Nelson's hounds found Byers' carcass. Buried up in Devil's Canyon. Hounds sniffed aroun' an' started diggin' and there's Byers, dead as a doornail."

"What was Old Wolf doin' in Devil's?"

"Coyotee huntin', he claims. He saw the hounds diggin' an' he got off his cayuse an' dug with 'em to see what they was trying to dig up an' when he saw Byers' face I guess he almos' kicked the bucket, he got so scared."

"He drunk, as usual?"

"Naturally. Ol' Wolf went completely nuts. He beats his cayuse hell-fer-leather into town for the sheriff. Doc Estambre's got Ol' Wolf doped up now so he sleeps."

Dee scowled. "Well, one thing for certain, Shorty. They cain't accuse me of murderin' Byers."

"Who do you figger kilt him?" Shorty asked.

"I don't know. I figured Byers as jobbin' me to make it look like I killed Craig while all the time he did it an' robbed Craig. Now I got to think of somethin' different."

"He was burned."

Dee studied his hired hand. "Burned?"

"Yeah, burned. Fingers burned way back. Bottoms of his feet blistered an' burnt."

"Nobody tol' me that."

"I heard Doc Estambre say it hisself to the sheriff. Now why the heck would he be burned?"

"I can guess. He knew somethin'. Somebody else wanted to know what he knew. Byers wouldn't tell. So somebody gave him the ol' Sioux flame treatment."

"Somebody? Who's somebody?"

"That's what I wish I knew. I got a hunch there's more to this than meets the eye, Shorty."

"Explain, boss."

"Me, I still figure Byers killed Craig. He got Craig's money. He hid it somewhere an' acted normal like ridin' back to the herd an' all that."

Shorty nodded, faded blue eyes serious.

"Byers worked for somebody who wanted me outa the way an' saw a chance to lay Craig's killin' on me. Then Byers backed out an' decided to keep the money an' whoever paid him to kill Craig wanted that money."

"I getcha now, Dee. They toasted Byers hands an' feet. He finally told where the money was hid. Then they killed him."

"I'd say that was it, Shorty."

"An' jes' by accident, Byers' carcass was found. I'd say whoever kilt him was in a hurry or they'd have dug a deeper grave."

46

"That's as good a theory as any," Dee said.

"Let's say that Byers had Craig's money. Do you think he tol' where he had it hid?"

"I do. And I'll tell you why. Ol' Art says Byers was shot through the forehead by a pistol so close it left powder-burns. They wouldn't have killed him if he hadn't talked."

Shorty scratched his head. "We're jus' supposin' a lot but we ain't got nothin' concrete to work on, boss. Things ain't good outside for you. There's lots of hangtree talk in the Diamon' Willow."

"Millie tol' me the same."

Shorty glanced at Art Finnegan, leaning against the outside bars and listening. Finnegan did not see the significant look the cowhand shot toward the cell's only window.

"Later, Shorty," Dee murmured. "We'll see, amigo."

"What about the ranch, Dee? I need another hand."

"Mack Weston hit me up for a job at the dance. He's got a shack on the south edge of town."

"I know where it is. What'll I offer him?"

"The usual. Forty an' found. He's a good hand. Give him a deal for all winter an' he might go for thirty."

"Okay. See you."

Nancy Craig entered as Shorty left. Old Art Finnegan said, "Jus' like directin' traffic out in the street."

Dee found himself making a mental comparison of Millie and Branch Craig's daughter. Both were beauties— one blonde, one dark haired, but there similarity ended.

One was wealthy, educated. The other was a saloon-woman, nothing more. Millie had apparently been on her own since childhood. Nancy had been spoon-fed by her parents. Still, she had character, just as Millie had.

"What're you doin' here?" Dee asked.

"Dee, why do you always— Oh, I'll say it: Rub me the wrong way!"

"I'm sorry," Dee said. "I'm not myself." He shook his cell-gate noisily. "Monkey in a cage. In the zoo."

"Are you getting plenty to eat?"

"Yes, thanks to Millie."

"I heard she's been feeding you. Laura told me, in the Cafe. Nice you have a steady girl."

"Now who's jabbin' in the needle?"

"I'm not myself, either. They're burying Dad at the ranch today, next to mother. Reverend Astor will conduct the funeral. At two, Dee."

Tears filled her eyes. Dee's heart went out to her. He put his hands over hers gripping the cell-bars. She had lost both parents within a few months.

"I'm so sorry, Nancy."

"I think sometimes you killed Dad, and then other times I think different. I don't know what to think. I'm all confused."

"You've got company," Dee assured.

She withdrew her hands slowly. "Is there anything I can do, Dee?"

"Blow up this joint. Put dynamite under a corner an' blow out the boulders an' let me escape."

Art Finnegan said sternly, "Drop that talk, Bowden!"

Dee said, "Utterly without a sense of humor. What a terrible way to go through life."

Nancy studied him. "You don't seem worried."

"What's there to be worried about? I never murdered your father. They know damn' well I never killed Byers. I was here safe an' soun' in this cell when Byers got killed."

"What is this all about, Dee?"

"I gotta hunch, but I ain't sayin' it."

"I'd best go. I came in to buy some flowers from Mrs. Hanson. She's the only one around here with a rose garden and her roses are almost done for the year."

"You goin' teach school?"

"I don't know. I might have to stay home and run Rafter V. Your English is terrible. You drop all your g's."

"Jus' so they don't drop me six feet with a rope aroun' my neck. We get goin' good an' then you say somethin' like that."

"Goodbye." Stiffly.

"So long." With a grin.

Nancy left, back straight. Within ten minutes wide-shouldered Mark Stratton, sporting a new tailor-made gray suit, stood before Dee's cell. "Anything I can do for you, Bowden?"

"Fin' the guy that ambushed Craig."

Stratton smiled. "That I can't do. The sheriff's working on that. I brought you a cold bottle of beer."

Stratton took a bottle of Old Wyoming from a paper sack. Art Finnegan said, "He ain't allowed booze, Mr. Stratton."

"I'll be held responsible," Stratton said shortly.

The jailer hesitated, then remained silent. Dee opened the bottle with his teeth, spitting out the cork. "Might nice of you," he said. "My throat is parched."

The bottle rose, the beer feel.

"That didn't last long," Stratton said.

Dee wiped his lips with the back of his hand. "Your girl friend comes an' visits me," he said.

"My girl friend?"

"Millie."

Stratton laughed. "She's no 'count to me. She jes' works in my place. She must like you. She even run out after the sheriff. Wish she'd cotton to me like she does you."

"Everybody said she was your woman."

"Everybody was wrong. Your lawyer is working for you. He went to Cheyenne this morning."

Dee nodded. "Wonder who killed Byers?"

Stratton shrugged expensively-clad big shoulders. "Who knows? A man makes a heap of enemies in his life."

Dee found himself disliking this suave, oily individual. Stratton was a massive spider neither toiling or beneficial. Why had he come to visit him? Dee put the question into words.

"Friendly visit, nothing more, Bowden. Well, have to get moving. I'm your friend. This talk— Well, it's not good. But I'm not involved in it. I want you to know that.

I try to kill it every time I can in the Diamond Willow."

"I thank you," Dee assured.

Stratton's big back moved to the door and out of sight. Within minutes, the lanky, tall form of banker John Hendricks entered with old Art Finnegan grumbling, "Lord, another visitor."

Dee Bowden found himself instinctively disliking John Hendricks as much as he had disliked Mark Stratton. Here was another spider parasite who did not toil for his daily bread.

"Thought I'd drop in to see if I can do anything for you, Bowden." Hendricks put his rifle down, butt foremost, to shake hands.

Old Art Finnegan immediately grabbed the rifle. "That was in his reach, Mr. Hendricks! Damn it, I'm gettin' ol' an' forgetful! I should've had you hand over thet rifle afore I allowed you in!"

"Sorry, Mr. Finnegan," the banker said.

Hendricks' grip was strong. "Everything is in order, Mr. Bowden. Your debt to my bank is paid in full, the balance deposited in your checking account. Fortunately, the cattle-buyer paid your man, Shorty Messenger, in currency—thus no check had to be signed. Here are your receipts."

Dee glanced at the papers. One was his note. Scrawled across it was *Paid in Full*. He had a little over three thousand in his checking account. The thought came that Lawyer Dave Rutherman's bill would cut deeply into that account. This double-cross was costing him money.

And it might cost him his life, a dull voice inside said.

"Can I help you in any way, Mr. Bowden?"

"Blow this joint up under my boots. Get me outa here."

The lanky scarecrow showed a small smile. "I can hardly do that. First, I'm a legal-living citizen. That would be a crime. And, besides, you might get killed in the explosion."

"Bowden is plumb crazy," Finnegan said.

Hendricks said, "I leave you now." Then he, too, was

50

gone. Dee sat down on the concrete ledge and, for want of something to do, carefully scanned the bank's papers. All was in order there.

He'd give Shorty these papers to take to Diamond inside a Diamond. A sudden lonely feeling hit him, for he thought of his home-ranch, snuggled there on a curve in Beaver Creek.

He was lonesome. He put his head in his hands. He could joke and wisecrack in front of others but when alone he had to face himself—and he was scared deep inside. He was in a rough situation. He might not come out of it alive. That fact stared him in the face all the time.

"Headache?" Finnegan asked.

Dee didn't answer. He swung around to lie on the cot. Futility beat at him. What—oh, what—could he do?

Lawyer Rutherman . . . in Cheyenne? Trying to see the territorial governor. He sat up suddenly. Another visitor had entered. He was surprised to see Dave Rutherman.

"Thought you went to Cheyenne?"

Rutherman shook his head. "That was just a blind, Dee. I knew if I wired out of here the depot operator would tell everybody he knew what my wire contained."

"That's right. He's a gossipy gent."

Rutherman had gone down the line fifty miles to Wild Horse Junction and wired the governor from there. "An' what did you fin' out?" Dee asked hopefully.

"Nothing solid, Dee. Just that he'd look into your case. I pointed up legal point after legal point. His secretary took them down, the operator in Wild Horse said."

"You point out that the j. p. here—an' the county attorney—were ol' time buddies of Branch Craig?"

"That I did. Frankly, I told the governor you were being framed on merely circumstantial evidence—and that is the truth."

Dee rubbed his whiskery jaw. "Only one thing wrong, Attorney. Craig an' the governor were old friends. When Craig went each winter to the legislature he bunked at the governor's house."

"A governor still has to uphold his oath of office."

"Maybe yes, maybe no. You goin' to Craig's funeral?"

"I am. Sound out the temper of things."

Dave Rutherman left. Round Rock became very quiet. Dee judged almost all citizens had gone north to Rafter V and the funeral services. Shorty Messenger came in at five.

"Good lord, Dee! First, they wanted to tar an' feather him—just because of you—"

Dee sat up on his concrete slab. "What're you talkin' about?"

"They put him on his hoss! They pointed the hoss north toward Blasted Stone! They tol' him if'n he ever come back they'd kill him on sight!"

"Who'd they do this to?"

"Your lawyer— Dave Rutherman!"

Chapter Six

Dee gripped the bars. All this had happened, of course, at Branch Craig's funeral. Shorty's back was to Art Finnegan and therefore the jailer did not notice Shorty's suggestive look at the barred cell-window.

Dee slightly nodded.

Shorty said he had to go to Diamond inside a Diamond to do the chores. Yes, he had hired Mack Weston, who would start work Monday. "Thirty five per an' found."

Shorty left and Dee returned to his concrete. This would be his fourth night in this cell. He corrected this. It *might* be his fourth night. If this lynch talk grew stronger—and a lynch mob stormed the jail—

Old Art went out for supper. He came back with a worried face. Townsmen and Rafter V cowpunchers were doing heavy drinking in the Diamond Willow. "I don't like the way things are shapin' up, Bowden."

Dee's grin hid a fear he dared not show. "Can't do no more than lynch me," he told the ancient.

"I'm goin' talk to Sher'ff Watson."

The oldster shook the cell-door of Dee's cell, saw it was firmly locked, then went out the outer door, shaking it to test its lock, also—and Dee was alone in the cell.

Finnegan returned in some ten minutes. "What'd Watson say?" Dee asked. "Am I goin' be a guest of honor at a necktie party?"

"Best I don't tell you, Bowden."

"My neck, not yours."

"All right, here goes. Watson is worried. He's doin' all he can to quiet the talk but ain't got no luck. He is afraid to try to sneak you outa town 'cause he's bein' watched, he claims."

Dee nodded, throat dry.

Stratton an' Hendricks is also tryin' to talk sense to them fools. Let's hope they succeed, boy."

Dee Bowden scowled. He meant nothing to the saloon-keeper and the banker except as a customer to an occasional beer and a checking-account in Hendricks' bank.

And if he were lynched, Hendricks would undoubtedly fall heir to the three thousand he had in Hendricks' bank. And Mark Stratton surely wouldn't miss the money a now-and-then beer took in.

Their laboring in his behalf didn't make sense. He mentioned this fact to his jailer.

"Them two's civic-minded men," Art Finnegan said. "They're ag'in lawlessness an' disorder."

"You talk loco," Dee growled. "All Stratton needs to do to stop lynch-talk is run them all out of the Diamon' Willow an' close the door an' there'd be no other place they could get booze an' the talk'd soon die down."

"That's right. I never thought of that."

Dee sat on his bunk, fear running through him—and growing minute by minute in direct ratio to the rise in the babble of lynch-tree voices. By now Shorty would be heading back into Round Rock with a wagon and a team of stout horses pulling it—and some lengths of log-chain in the wagon box.

All depended on Shorty.

By nine a crowd began forming in front of the court-house, most of its members drunk. Sheriff Isaac Watson had never before had such a thing happen as an attempted jail-delivery.

He held off the crowd as well as he could. He attempted

54

to deputize some of the leaders but they refused to take the oath. Mark Stratton and John Hendricks were not in the group. They stayed in the Diamond Willow.

Old Art Finnegan tested Dee's cell-door to see it was firmly locked. It was. He then went out the jail's front door, clanging it hard to make sure it, too, was locked.

He then went to the front to aid his boss.

Old Art was surprised to discover that some of the town's most sedate matrons were in the mob. At nine-thirty the sheriff sent a townswoman to the Diamond Willow for Mark Stratton and John Hendricks.

"We need help desperately, Mrs. Jones. An' they're about the only sober men in town."

Mrs. Jones scurried away, ample bottom bobbing. Stratton and Hendricks came with double-barreled sawed-off shotguns Stratton kept in the Diamond Willow, but neither the men—or the weapons—scared the roiling mob.

"Hit from the alley!" a man screamed.

"No, no! We need every manjack in front!"

By ten, the mob acted. Sheriff Watson and his deputies went down under the surging mass of drunken, irate humanity.

A fist sent the sheriff reeling backward. He landed on his rump, disappearing under the hurrying boots. Old Art went down, too, but Stratton and Hendricks merely ran, shotguns unfired.

The saloonman and banker then watched from the crowd's perimeter, shotguns discreetly pointing downward. Boots and shoes pounded the dust toward the jail.

Kerosene torches cast flickering lights across ghastly, strained human faces. Screaming and cursing tore from human throats. The mob had gone berserk.

"A rope, a rope!"

A catchrope was thrown over the heads of the mob to its leaders. Quickly it was tied around the jail's outer door. A cowboy took his dallies around saddle-horn, then spurred his bronc ahead.

The bronc hit the end of the rope. The steel door held. Again, the cowpony lunged—this time, the door was ripped from iron hinges. The mob stormed inside.

"He murdered the bes' man this range has ever produced!"

"He'll pay, the bastard!"

"He's in the first cell. Here, Sig—that torch. Hold it higher. For god's sake, he's not there!"

"Look in the other cell? He's got to be here!"

"He ain't there, either!"

"Hey, look! The bars— On the window— They're ripped out an' even the concrete—"

"He's had help from the alley!"

"Where's that man who said not to watch the alley? Oh, here you are, huh, Matt? Take this for a present!"

A hard-knuckled fist slammed out. It crashed into Matt's face. Matt went reeling back. Another fist came from nowhere, knocked the town boot-maker flat.

"Get your hosses, men! We got to run him down!"

The mob broke up immediately. Boots hurried homeward for saddle-horses. Sheriff Isaac Watson climbed laboriously to his boots, blood on his sunken jaw. "This job wasn't meant for me," he mourned to the world in general.

"Shorty Messenger," Art Finnegan gasped. "He's come in through the alley, jerked the bars loose— I never seen him do it, but I know he did!"

Stratton and Hendricks said nothing.

The sheriff said, "Thanks for your help. I'm glad none of us fired. It would have been useless. Jes' killed some other men an' this grass has seen enough dead men to last it a long time."

"You're right, sheriff," Stratton said. And then, to Hendricks, "Let's go to the saloon, John, and have a drink, huh?"

"I need one," John Hendricks said.

"How about me?" Art Finnegan asked.

"Come along," Stratton told the jailer. "Always room

for another. Sheriff, how about you?"

"I got to ask some questions."

Stratton, Hendricks and Art disappeared in the starlight, leaving the sheriff alone with his wife and the oldest six of their twelve. "You all right, papa?" a ten year old daughter asked.

"I'm all right. First prisoner I ever lost."

"First murder-prisoner you ever had," the sheriff's fat wife reminded. "When me an' the kids hurried over here we saw Shorty Messenger enter town with a team hitched to a lumber-wagon."

"Why didn't you tell me?"

"You never asked."

"Everybody's got a right to enter this town," said an eleven year old boy. "I learned that in school last year."

"I'd best get my horse," the sheriff said. "This thing ain't finished yet. You got home, mama, and put on the coffee, huh?"

The Watson clan disappeared into the starlight. Sheriff Isaac Watson hurried to the town livery barn. Dee Bowden had his buckskin stabled there. To his surprise, a lumber-wagon and team were tied to the Mercantile's hitchrack, with Shorty Messenger sitting on the high spring seat.

"They kill Dee, sheriff?"

"He escaped."

"Escaped? How?"

"You ask me how? Hell, you know how. You pulled the bars off'n the winder."

"Can you prove that? Did you see such?"

"No, I didn't."

"Anybody else report such?" Shorty Messenger's voice was calm and steady. Sheriff Isaac Watson hesitated, then said, "Nobody reported such."

"Then quit throwin' such my way, sheriff."

Watson tugged his left mustache. "Guess I'm nutty tonight like the rest of this burg. Good lord, even the Ladies Aid was in the mob hollerin' to lynch Dee!"

Shorty grinned. "Had they lynched him I mighta been the heir to Diamond in a Diamond, seein' Dee ain't got a close relative in this world. He done tol' me that."

"You ain't seen Dee, have you?"

"Not since I visited him last in your jailhouse."

"Oh, hell! I mean ridin' his buckskin aroun' town tonight?"

"Yeah, I saw his buckskin just a few minutes ago. Couldn't make out who rid him, though."

"You did! Which way'd the bronc go?"

"North, toward Diamond in a Diamond, but like I said—"

But Sheriff Watson was gone on the run. Riders were streaming out of Round Rock heading north toward Diamond inside a Diamond, steelshod hoofs kicking dust behind to lay pale and yellow in the starlight.

Sheriff Watson thundered past, plying his shotloaded quirt hard to his bay's laboring ribs. His fast horse soon caught up with the posse. Within a short distance—right opposite Wolf Nelson's shack—they caught up with Dee Bowden's trotting buckskin.

Mack Weston turned the horse around to meet the posse. "What the tarnation's goin' on?"

"How come you're on Dee Bowden's hoss?" Sheriff Watson demanded.

"Shorty Messenger tol' me to ride him out to Diamon' inside a Diamon', sheriff. I wanted no part of that mob in front of your jail an' besides I shoved my schedule ahead."

Sheriff Watson studied the wide, whiskery face. "What'd you mean by shovin' your schedule ahead, Mack?"

"I was goin' out to Diamon' inside a Diamon' to work next week. Winter job. But when Shorty asked me if I'd ride Sonny out— Where you all headin' for?"

A man said, "We aim to burn down Diamon' inside a Diamon'"

Mack Weston stood on stirrups and looked at the man. "Why burn down them buildin's? Them buildin's ain't done you no harm."

A townsman said, "Hell, Dee Bowden won't be at his ranch! He ain't that much of a fool. Wonder if ol' Wolf has run off anythin' lately?" He looked at Wolf Nelson's shack. "Lissen to them damn' hounds yammer! 'Nuff to wake up a dead man—"

"I'm powerful dry," a man said.

They all rode to the wolfer's shack. Old Wolf Nelson was dead, all right—dead drunk. He lay on his back on the floor snoring through slack lips. Mingled with his natural stink of unwashed body and coyote scent he reeked of rawhide whiskey.

Evidently he had just bottled a batch for rows of bottles—all filled and glistening under the cabin's kerosene light—covered the rickety old table. Eager hands went out. Eager fingers curled around necks of bottles. Eager teeth pulled out corks.

Eager throats met plunging liquid fire. "Ah," a man breathed. "Sheriff, you'll have to catch Bowden without me. This is a paradise."

"Good booze," a man said.

Sheriff Watson breathed in relief. He had had visions of seeing the prosperous Diamond within a Diamond going up in flames, a complete waste of valuable property that would have been another mark against his so-far flawless lawman record.

Somebody shoved uncorked bottle into the lawman's hands. Sheriff Watson just held it to be accomodating. Mack Weston had ridden Dee's buckskin north into the night.

"I'm goin' bed down here tonight," one man said. "I've got a terrible headache."

"Stratton's rotgut. He shouldn't ship in whiskey. He oughta get ol' Wolf here to make his booze for 'im."

Watson said, "Territorial statutes prohibit a man makin' his own alcohol, men."

Somebody laughed. "Then why don't you close ol' Wolf's still down, sheriff?"

"I don't work for the Territory. I work for the county." Sheriff Watson saw the dim outlines of a lumber-wagon coming. He walked out the few paces to the road.

"I forgot to look in your wagon-box, Shorty."

Shorty Messenger pulled in his team. "Look all you wanna, sheriff. I got a few cans of tomatoes in that box, the reason I druv into town. Dee ordered me to buy them."

"What's under that tarp?"

"Pick it up an' look for yourself, sheriff."

Sheriff Watson lifted the canvas tarp. Under it was only the slivery wagon-box bottom.

"Could I ask you what you're lookin' for, Sheriff Watson?"

"A chain?"

Shorty Messenger laughed shortly. "What t'hell would I be doin' with a chain, sheriff?"

"Pullin' out window bars."

"Why don't you arrest me, sheriff? I need a long, long rest at county expense. Roundin' up thet last bunch of Diamon' in a Diamon' dogies plumb wore me out. I could stand a rest."

"Drive on," Sheriff Watson said sourly.

Chapter Seven

Dee Bowden slept little the remainder of that fate-filled night. For one thing, the hay in the haymow of old Jake Spooner's Town Livery Barn was filled with foxtail grass. The foxtail barbs kept working into his clothing and pricking his skin.

Also, were he to sink into a sound sleep he might snore and betray his hiding place to horsemen coming and going in the barn below. For he was now a hunted man—a jail-breaker charged with murder. Eternal vigilance would be in order from now until he cleared his name.

And how would he do that?

Lying hidden under the loose hay, the rough boards of the haymow under him, he gave deep thought to his predicament to this moment—and finding the proceedings pleasing to a very small degree.

He owed it all to Shorty Messenger, a stout team and a length of heavy steel chain. The only point about this jail-break that bothered him was that perhaps somebody had seen Shorty at work.

Where was Shorty Messenger now? In jail for bringing about the successful jail-delivery?

This question soon found answer. Two town matrons entered below to check on the horses there enstabled to see if their spouses had indeed ridden out of Round Rock.

Their words came clearly upward for the haymow floor had wide cracks in it. Evidently the planks had been

61

green when nailed into place but when dried out had shrunk.

"Both of their horses are gone," Mrs. Burnham told Mrs. Morgan. "Did you know that Shorty Messenger was discovered on Main Street by Sheriff Watson himself, with Shorty settin' in the Diamond in a Diamond lumber wagon, his horses doin' nothin'.'."

"My lan' an' heavens alive! Sheriff Watson arrest him?"

"No, he let him drive outa town. He had no evidence against Shorty. Mrs. Watson tol' me thet herself."

"Mrs. Watson's due to have another baby soon, ain't she?"

"Aroun' Christmas, she told me."

"Good lands an' heavens alive! When they gonna quit?"

"You gotta ask them, Missus Morgan." And Dee Bowden heard heavy-set Mrs. Burnham snicker. "Evidently they like it, huh?"

"I'd say so. Now my Jacob an' me...." The female voices trailed off and out the wide front door.

Dee grinned. He was sure nobody had seen him climb up into the haymow. The barn had been without humans except old Jake Spooner, the owner—and Jake had slept in his cubicle in his easy-chair, head hanging with mouth agape as he snored in drunken bliss.

Dee's first impulse, after scrambling out the ruined cell-window, was to get Sonny from the livery and ride hell-for-leather for his Diamond inside a Diamond, but common sense had soon killed that plan.

Townsmen would ride immediately to his spread and look for him there. Suddenly, he had decided the best place for him to hide was here in town—and in the loose hay of the Town Livery Barn.

"You get Mack Weston. Have him ride Sonny out to the home-ranch, Shorty. Then you act natural on Main Street, like you'd just driv into town for supplies, or somethin' like that."

"Hanson's ol' lady's got the Merc open, I noticed as I drove in. I'll buy a case or so of tomaters there to make it look good. We kin always use tomaters on the ranch."

"Good idea. Put them on the Diamond in a Diamond charge there."

"Wonder if anybody saw me?"

"Had anybody seen us they'd have been shootin'."

Shorty smiled. "Easiest jail-break I ever did, boss. You go to Spooner's barn an' me an' this rig out on Main Street. Where an' when'll I see you again, boss?"

"That drift fence we strung across the mouth of Moccasin Canyon to keep our dogies from wanderin' into the badlands— Day after tomorrow, I'll meet you there."

"If they watch me too close I'll not come."

Dee crawled under the canvas tarp inside the wagon. The wagon lumbered away. Shorty stopped once to hide the chain under the Mercantile's store-room, then drove on again.

"Spooners," he intoned, "an' nobody on the street."

Dee left the protection of the tarp. He swung down to the ground, glancing left and right, seeing nobody—and darted into the back door of the stable, the good smell of manure and hay and horseflesh in his nostrils.

Within seconds, he had ascended the ladder to the haymow and dug himself a hiding place in the loose hay. He clutched a Winchester .30-30 rifle. Extra .30-30 cartridges were in his pockets.

A broad gunbelt, loaded with brass-shiny .45 shells, was a comforting weight around his slim hips, his extra .45 Colt riding on his right thigh, thanks to Shorty Messenger.

All he now needed was a horse. And below him were stout horses munching hay and oats. Soon more broncs would be stabled below when the irate lynch mob returned. He could have his pick.

He'd not pick a cream-colored buckskin though. Any man riding a light-colored buckskin on this range would be under immediate surveillance and run down to earth to make sure that rider was not one Dee Bowden astraddle his buckskin, Sonny.

Peace entered Dee Bowden's soul. Although still a hunted man with a murder charge hanging over his blond head, he at least had his freedom—if only for a limited length of time.

He swore he'd never surrender alive. He'd fight until he was killed before he'd allow himself again taken prisoner.

Never for one moment did he think of abandoning his home Diamond in a Diamond range. Although not born in this Round Rock area it had been his home all his life, and he would stay in this area until he died a natural death—or fell dead under a long rifle shot or a gunfight with shortguns.

Common sense told him the county would post a big reward for his capture, dead or alive. Without knowing it, he sank into a fitful slumber to be awakened by two things—voices below and hunger inside.

"Why you saddlin' your hoss, Stratton?"

"He's goin' out for a mornin' hossback ride," another man said.

Both speakers had coarse voices, Dee noticed— whiskey-loaded heaviness. He listened carefully, ear over a wide crack. Had they burned down his precious Diamond in a Diamond buildings he had labored and saved to construct? His heart was heavy.

Stratton said, "Heading out for a horseback ride, like Mutt here said. You boys burn down Bowden's spread?"

Both drunks laughed heartily. "We never got no further than Wolf Nelson's shack. We caught Bowden's buckskin. Who the hell you suppose sat the hoss's saddle?"

"Who?" Stratton asked.

"Mack Weston. He's goin' work this winter for Bowden. Shorty Messenger is his boss an' Shorty ordered Mack to ride Dee's hoss out to Diamon' inside a Diamon'. They caught Bowden yet?"

"Ain't seen hide nor hair of him."

"We sampled Nelson's booze. Damn, he makes good

'shine. How come you don't buy your hard liquor off'n him, Stratton?"

"Law won't let me. I got to buy licensed stuff."

"I gotta git home," one townsman said. "My wife'll skin me alive, drunk as I is!"

"And me for open range," Stratton said.

Bootheels departed. Soon a horse left the barn. Dee glanced out the corner of the cobweb-draped haymow window. Stratton rode north, bit and tough in his expensive, hand-carved leather.

Dee scowled. Well, Diamond inside a Diamond was still standing. He had deliberately picked a good listening-post. More drunken riders came in. All proclaimed to the world the excellence of old Wolf Nelson's whiskey.

Dee learned that Dave Rutherman had left the country. He'd hurriedly packed his duds and climbed on the stage heading out of Blasted Stone, swearing never to return to such a land of gun-hung and gun-crazy idiots.

"Cowboy ridin' down from Blasted Stone tol' me this," the man below said. "Said Rutherman sure was in a hurry."

Dee Bowden, hidden above, had a moment of sardonic glee. With Rutherman gone he'd not have to pay the attorney for services rendered ... that is, if Rutherman had rendered any help.

Three men bought bottles to Spooner. "Compliments of ol' Wolf," one said. Spooner immediately began sampling each. When Dee sneaked down, Spooner was again sleeping in his chair in his cubicle, mouth open to show brown tobacco-colored teeth.

Dee found one saddle with a can of beans in its bag. Another held some hard biscuits. Dee then had his lunch upstairs. An hour later a cowboy came in looking for his beans.

The cowboy accused Spooner of stealing his beans. Spooner called him a liar, saying he'd had no beans. "Stiffs like you, Garrison, drive me to drink."

"I'd beat the hell outa you for a common thief,"

Garrison growled, "if you wasn't so damn' old."

"Come on," Spooner invited.

Garrison laughed sardonically and left.

They buried Hank Byers that afternoon at two. The cemetery was south of Round Rock a half-mile. Most of the town walked the distance. Dee watched from the haymow window.

Business establishments closed for the services. Hank Byers in death had gained a popularity he plainly had not owned in life. Once again the cowtown became silent for another funeral.

During this period, Dee Bowden stole a bay horse from the broncs stabled below. Even old Spooner had wobbled his way to the graveyard. Dee had all the time in the world.

He selected a good Hamley saddle from the kaks thrown over the rails. He jammed his Winchester .30-30 into the empty leather saddle-boot. Coiled over the kak's fork was a new thirty-five foot Manila hardtwist rope. He swung the leather on the bay, caught the cinch.

Within minutes, he rode out the barn's rear door. He found the alley and headed north. He prayed nobody would see him leave Round Rock. His prayer, though, was not answered.

The town bootmaker had not gone to Byers funeral. The blow he'd been handed in the face had given him two black eyes. He had not wanted to be seen in public.

He hoed his garden when Dee turned the corner. He stared, a bunch of radishes in hand, for Dee was only a few rods away.

The bootmaker dropped his radishes. "Dee Bowden! An' in the flesh— Myra, my rifle! Five thousand dollars on his head an'—"

He never finished. Dee's Winchester had suddenly left the saddle-boot. The barrel flashed down as Dee spurred his stolen bronc forward. The hard steel hit the bootmaker on the head.

The man screamed, went down. Dee fed his bronc the

spurs, riding twisted in saddle, rifle on the fallen man.

The bootmaker kept hollering for his wife—and his rifle. Dee rounded the corner, bay kicking dust behind. A level stretch of sagebrush lay ahead, for he was beyond Round Rock's limits.

He laid his hooks to the hard-running bay. He had some quarter-mile of sagebrush covered distance to traverse until safe in the hills. Suddenly he saw sand spurt upward in a small geyser thirty feet ahead and slightly to his right.

He knew, without looking back, that somebody had shot at him with a rifle. Reins tied around saddlehorn, he twisted on stirrups, Winchester rising. A woman stood at the alley's exit, rifle to her shoulder.

He saw the rifle spout smoke. This time the lead made a geyser closer, and to his left. He raised his rifle. He triggered once, shooting at the shed at the woman's left.

He wanted to scare, not kill. But his bullet, if it landed even close, failed in its purpose. This time the rifle-lead hit a rod behind his running horse.

Fear hit him. The woman was a good shot. She was getting her range. Her next bullet—

Then, the bay hit a coulee. He smashed through bullberry and buckbrush and he and rider were hidden. Dee heard a bullet ricochet in whining anger from a nearby boulder.

He knew this coulee well for he'd rawhided many a horn-swinging Diamond inside a Diamond steer from its brush-filled area. He followed a dim trail ground into the flinty soil by cattle and deer that twisted upward to end a mile to the northwest on a brush-covered mesa.

Suddenly, the bay shied.

Automatically, Dee's Winchester rose, then fell as he saw that a white-tailed doe, leaping from the rosebushes ahead, had startled his mount. The deer bounced over the rim and out of sight.

Had the doe been a buck, he'd been down by now—for fresh venison appealed to Dee Bowden's empty stomach.

Dee reached the mesa. There, hidden in high brush, he looked back down on Round Rock, a dim dot in distance, the ribs of his stolen horse rising and falling sharply under his stirrup-leathers.

He remembered the bootmaker screaming, "Five thousand dollars on his head—!" He gave his situation brief but penetrating analysis.

Round Rock would now know he had ridden northwest. Round Rock would send out a posse to hunt him down. Five thousand dollars was more than most cowpunchers earned in a lifetime.

More than a posse under Sheriff Ike Watson would hunt for him. Individuals, spurred by five thousand dollars, would seek his life or capture.

He summed up points. Five thousand, dead or alive... preferably dead. Horse stealing charge, and on this range they hanged horse-thieves. Yes, and a bigger, more terrible accusation.

Murder....

Chapter Eight

Shorty Messenger trimmed side-branches from a young pine destined to become a corral rail when Nancy Craig rode into Diamond inside a Diamond, her pinto gelding tossing his head against the curb bit.

"Thought you'd be in town for Byers' funeral," Shorty said.

"Byers meant nothing to me."

"You're purty, Nancy. But Dee's got another jus' as purty."

"That saloon hussy—Millie—?"

Shorty's sharp double-bitted axe snipped a branch free. "I refer to none other. How come you ride out so far from Rafter V? Dee ain't on these premises."

"Where is he?"

"I dunno. An' if'n I did know, I'd not tell nobody. Maybe you rid over to visit with me?"

"You flatter yourself."

Shorty grinned. "A bad habit I got, my sixth wife told me. Jes' as she was packin' to leave, she said the same. What the tarnation's arrivin' from the south? A win'storm throwin' up thet much dust? Or is them riders hailing out from Round Rock?"

Nancy looked. "Riders. Your English is worse even than Dee's. He always drops his g's. You mangle up every other word."

"My fourth wife tol' me the same. She was a

schoolmarm. Strange thing, though—people seem to understand me. Our honorable lawman, Sir Isaac Watson, heads them riders, it 'pears to me."

The horseman thundered into the Diamond inside a Diamond yard to pull in with sliding-hoofs that raised a cloud of yellow dust that the endless prairie wind soon swept aside.

For some reason, Shorty Messenger found himself checking on Mark Stratton, who was not in the group, and his eyes moved over to tall John Hendricks, who sat a sweaty blue roan stud, his .25-20 rifle jammed stock upward in the hand-carved leather saddle-boot.

Shorty doffed his old Stetson. He held the old black hat over his heart as he gazed up soulfully into the wizened face of Sheriff Watson. "Your Honor," he intoned. "I am not guilty."

"Guilty of what?" the sheriff snapped.

"Of whatever you are about to accuse me of."

Sheriff Watson pulled his right mustache. "It's bad enough to deal with the sane let alone the locos. Dee Bowden jus' rode out of town on Jim North's top saddler, havin' stole same from Spooner's barn."

Shorty stared upward as though in surprise, remembering he was supposed to meet Dee tomorrow in Moccasin Canyon. "Did you shoot him from horse?" he asked.

The lawman shifted his weight on his Visalia stirrups. "Good lord, if we had do you figure we'd have rid out this far for to tell you? No, he got away. Mrs. Vazquez—the bootmaker's wife—shot at him but apparently missed. He knocked her husband cold."

"That's good. He made a bad pair of boots for me an' would never make good on 'em. I almost come to the point of cold-cockin' him myself. Which direction did Dee go?"

"Northwest."

Shorty shrugged. "You can look all over here for 'im

but you won't find 'im, sher'ff. Did he shoot back?"

"He did."

"Wonder where he got his weapon? Did he shoot with a shortgun or a Winchester?"

"Rifle. Mrs. Vasquez saw him clearly raise a rifle. Now the point is this: Where did he get that rifle?"

Shorty shrugged. "Why ask me? Maybe Dee snaked a rifle from a saddle-boot in Spooner's barn when he borrowed North's horse?"

"*Borrowed* my horse!" Burly Jim North's angry voice held threatening undertones. "Hell, Bowden stole my horse! An' on this range we hangs horsethieves!"

"Do tell," Shorty said. "Well, you can only hang a man once, I read somewhere sometime."

North glared at him. He spoke from the corner of his mouth to Sheriff Isaac Watson. "I tol' you this ride out here would be jus' wasted time! This cowpunch helped Bowden escape."

"Wait a minute, North—"

But irate Jim North interrupted the sheriff with, "You know that! So do I! Sure, there were not witness—but what the hell— Everybody knows him an' Bowden— Well, they're buddies. Arrest him, sheriff! Jug the little bastard!"

Shorty Messenger coldly studied the big man. "Are my ears hearin' right, North? Did you call me a *bastard*?"

"The name fits."

"I don't figger it does, North." Shorty raised his voice not an iota. "Besides, my mother an' father were legally married!"

Two forward strides, one leap—and Shorty Messenger bodily dragged the big man from saddle with a display of great muscular strength.

All was confusion. Horses reared, neighed, fought bits. North's riderless bronc fled, reins dragging.

"Hol' it, men!" yelled Sheriff Watson.

Watson might as well screamed into a tornado. North

could handle guns or fists. Later onlookers remembered they'd never before seen good-natured Shorty Messenger in action.

Shorty fought with great determination. His dead parents had been insulted. He had been grievously insulted, too.

Jim North had the rep of being one of the toughest men on Round Rock range. He could bulldog a steer with only one burly arm, a display of raw brutal strength.

He'd won many a fistfight in the Diamond Willow. He was fast, had a little science—and loved to fight.

Jim North got in two solid hits. His right fist thudded against Shorty's left jaw. North's second hit was when his wide bottom hit the Wyoming dust. Later onlookers said one short left jab from Shorty had dumped the tough guy.

And when North made his second hit, he was completely beat up. Shorty's left, always out, opened a cut here, another there, in the big face. Blood seeped from North's nose and mouth.

Shorty stood over his fallen foe in the best of John L. Sullivan stances. "Mebbe you want more, North?"

North shook his head. "I know when I'm bested."

"Am I a bastard?"

"You ain't, Shorty. You're folks was married. I remember now...."

Shorty extended a hand. He helped his bloody, beaten adversary to his boots. "Best go to the hoss trough an' wash up. They's a towel hangin' on the pump handle. Thanks for the fistic workout."

North tried to grin, couldn't. "You're welcome, Shorty."

Shorty reached into his mouth and tested a tooth. Nancy Craig asked, "Loose tooth?" and Shorty nodded, attention again on Sheriff Isaac Watson. "Go ahead an' search the ranch, sher'ff. Then git out, please. Nancy come to visit me, not the whul danged town of Round Rock."

Banker John Hendricks spoke for the first time.

"Bowden won't be here, sheriff. And if he was, he'd be hidden deep in some cellar or such. Sooner or later some rifle or shortgun will knock Bowden from horse. That is, if he don't pull out of the country for good."

"Five thousan' bucks is a lot of money," a townsman said.

Shorty asked, "Why's Jones mention five thousan' dollars, sher'ff?"

"Bounty money, Shorty. On Dee Bowden's head. Dead or alive."

Nancy Craig's face stiffened. Shorty said, "I'm goin' out huntin' my boss. I'll fin' him an' kill him. Five thousan' bucks— Man alive!"

"This whole thing is crazy," Nancy said. "Rafter V will put not a cent on Dee's head. There's no concrete evidence he ambushed and killed my father."

"Hoss stealin'," Sheriff Watson said gravely. "Hangin' offense, Miss Nancy. Was your father here he'd tell you the same."

"But he isn't here. He did a number of savage, evil things in his life. He wasn't a simon-pure. Oh, yes, he was my father—and I his only child, but that doesn't close my eyes, Sheriff Watson."

"Amen," the sheriff intoned.

Nancy and Shorty sat on the top corral rail of the horse corral while Sheriff Watson's men searched every nook and cranny of Diamond inside a Diamond. Finally the search was over. It had, of course, netted no Dee Bowden.

Sheriff Watson reined close, posse around him. "Thanks for the hospitality, Shorty."

"I might file suit against you," Shorty said. "You searched these premises without a search warrant, sher'ff—a point definitely ag'in the law."

Sheriff Watson tugged his right mustache. "Maybe I didn't need one. Are you a lawyer, Shorty?"

"I know that much law."

Sheriff Watson's face stiffened. "Don't sharp-horn me aroun', Shorty. I've taken a lot these last few days. I might arrest you here an' now for assaultin' Jim North."

"Well, well, now....." Shorty said. Then to North, "You want him to put me in irons for a fair an' up fistfight?"

North's good humor had returned. "Good lord no, Shorty. They'd laugh me outa Roun' Rock if'n I signed such a warrant. I got you outweighed by at least fifty pounds an' yet you beat the— Well, you whupped me, fair an' even."

Shorty looked at the sheriff. "That's your answer, sher'ff."

"Things ain't goin' right," Sheriff Watson said, and then added, "fer me, at least. They's another warrant out for Dee's arrest, too, you know."

"I didn't know," Shorty returned. "How does it read?"

"Assault an' battery. He knocked a reporter on his— Well, he knocked him down."

"More such parasites should be knocked flat," Shorty said.

"This reporter was for the *Star*, the territory's biggest newspaper. Lot of political power, the *Star*. An' the reporter— He's the territorial governor's nephew. Favorite nephew, they tells me."

Shorty said in make-believe tragedy, "Another black mark ag'in my boss's formerly good record. When an' if I see Dee I'll give him all the good news you brought, sher'ff."

Sheriff Watson's eyes grew small. "Mebbe you'll see Dee soon somewhere in the badlands?"

"You must want to make a long, long hossback ride, sheriff."

"Why did you say that?"

"'Cause you'd be trailin' me, sure as shootin'. Me, I don't like ginks hangin' on my backtrail. I shoot to kill 'em. I hole up an' get my Winchester an' I shoot the bast— I shoot from the saddle." The cowpuncher looked at Nancy. "Sorry I almost said a bad word, Miss Craig."

Nancy said, "I've heard such before. My father had

some choice adjectives and he'd spout them out regardless of where he was or who listened."

Sheriff Watson waved his right arm. "Let's ride outa this nest of locos, men!"

Spade bits wheeled plunging, rearing cayuses. Hard spur-rowels whammed equine ribs. And then the posse pounded south, apparently heading back to Round Rock, dust hanging high behind shod hoofs.

Hard-riding Wyoming saddlemen pounded leather. Banker John Hendricks rode on Sheriff Watson's right, ever-present rifle under his right saddle-fender. Jim North rode on the lawman's left.

Soon the posse was out of sight.

Chapter Nine

Shorty Messenger and Nancy Craig watched the posse disappear with Shorty gingerly feeling his bum tooth. "The banker was there but I didn't see the saloon-man," the cowpuncher said.

"Mark Stratton?"

"Yeah, Stratton."

Nancy related that when she had turned the milk cow out that morning she had seen a rider far west against the rimrock. "Since we started losing cattle, I've got the habit of putting my field glasses on every rider out early or late—and that one turned out to be Mark Stratton."

Shorty's brows rose.

"What he was doing out on the range that early in the morning I don't know, but he was riding toward the northwest. Hendricks rides out a lot early, too. I've seen him a number of times early in the morning."

Shorty came down from the corral rail. "Ol Wolf Nelson's snake-bite anteedote— In the bunkhouse— Care for a nip, Miss Nancy?"

Nancy followed him down. "Don't mind if I do, Shorty." She brushed the front of her buckskin riding-skirt. "Yonder— Direction of Round Rock— Rider coming, huh?"

Shorty peered. "You got good eyes. Long ways off. On the wagon road, headin' north. Prob'ly somebody headin' north fer Blasted Stone. County road, any taxpayer can use it. Ladies first, Miss Nancy."

Nancy entered the long log bunkhouse with its sod roof. It was glisteningly clean and there wasn't a woman on Diamond in a Diamond. She sat at the table while Shorty went to his knees, dug under his bunk, and came out with a bottle.

He swished the bottle's contents. "Clear as spring water, Miss Nancy." He pulled the cork with his teeth, then winced. "Hurt my bad tooth. Wish Dee was here an' things were like they was a week ago. I miss the bugger."

"I do, too. Nobody to argue with. No, I'll take it straight out of the bottle. How's your molar?" Nancy took a drink. She handed the bottle to Shorty.

"Might be busted in two." Shorty's rope-calloused hands loved the bottle.

Shorty soon tipped up a snort. Nancy decided on another drink. The moonshine was hot as Taos lightning, the whiskey of the trappers. Nancy had sampled it, too.

"Where's thet rider thet was comin'?" Nancy asked and added, "My lord, I'm getting to speak English like you do."

"You should loosen up now an' then. Here's to Dee, wherever my good pal Dee is, an' God bless his ornery soul."

"To Dee Bowden."

Nancy raised the bottle. She lowered it with, "Ah," and looked at its contents. "That bottle is a pint bottle, ain't it?"

"We've kilt half a pint, Miss Craig."

"Nancy's the name."

"I got more cached, Nancy. Hey, look! In the doorway—"

Millie stood in the door. She was beautiful and blonde just as Nancy was beautiful and brunette. She wore a buckskin riding shirt with decorative Sioux beadwork. Her blue silk blouse protruded womanly in the right places, just as did Nancy's green silk blouse.

"Oh, excuse me, please. Am I intruding?"

"Not a bit, Miss Millie," Shorty hurriedly said. "We're jes' exercisin' our drinkin' powers. Have a snort, young lady." Shorty gallantly extended the bottle. He realized he'd not eaten breakfast. He was getting loop-legged.

Strangely, Nancy now had no antagonism for what she considered her rival. "Maybe the lady wants a glass, Shorty?"

"No, no," Millie said. "I like it from the bottle. I was a bottle baby." All laughed at this seemingly uproarish joke. Millie lowered the bottle half an inch. "Good booze. That whiskey where I work—" She grimaced.

"You come out lookin' for Dee?" Nancy asked.

"Not particularly," Millie said. "I went out for a horseback ride. Then thought I'd ride out here to see Shorty and talk to him. Was that a posse I met?"

"Sheriff Isaac Watson searched the premises," Shorty said.

"I guess they never found Dee, 'cause he wasn't in the party." Suddenly Millie's face whitened. "They never found Dee—an'—?"

"No, they didn't fin' him," Shorty assured, "an' you can't hang a man you ain't got. You need another, Millie. You're kinda pale under the gills."

"I can stand another, too," Nancy said.

Shorty got down on his knees beside a bunk. "I'll get another bottle. Don't worry about the booze. I got four more bottles hid under there." He pulled another cork with his teeth. "Golly, that hurt my molar," he told Nancy.

"You'd best get that molar attended to," Nancy said. "There's a travelin' dentist that comes every month to Round Rock, you know."

Shorty grimaced. "I know. He drilled a hole in one of my teeth. He looked at his drill. The drill had gold flakes on it. He asked me if the tooth hadn't been filled before."

"Oh," Nancy said.

Millie drank deeply.

"I said no, it hadn't. Then where did the gold come from, he asks? I had a clean shirt on, one of them with a celluloid collar with a collar-button in the back."

"I remember," Nancy said. "Dorothy Thomas wedding, it was. You looked funny, all dolled up."

"I sure didn't feel funny. Well, get back to this dentist an' gold on his drill. I told him, 'Hell, you've drilled into my collar button!'"

Again, uproaring laugher. Millie demanded to know what had happened to Shorty's tooth. Shorty showed how he had whipped Jim North, shadow boxing, hitting grunting.

Nancy looked at Millie. "Let's look at his tooth, Millie?"

"Lay down, Shorty," Millie said.

Shorty lay on his back on his bunk. He opened his mouth wide. Both girls felt into the damp cavern and peered inside.

Millie said, "The tooth is broke."

"Broke in two," Nancy assured. "What'd you suppose become of the other half?"

"I must've swallered it in the combat. That tooth needs to come out," Shorty said.

Millie glanced significantly at Nancy. Nancy looked significantly at Millie. "I never pulled a tooth," Millie said.

"I've pulled hoss's teeth," Nancy said.

Shorty said, "Pinchers in the drawer over there. Best that thing is pulled. I'll prepare myself more, though." The bottle went up and half its contents spilled down Shorty's leathery throat. He lay back with a sigh, closed his eyes, opened his mouth. "Pull an' be danged, females."

The pinchers turned out to be heavy wire-cutter pliers. Nancy had a difficult time getting the tooth between the pincher's jaws for the pinchers were very big for such a small job.

"Need help?" Millie asked.

"No, I kin do it," Nancy replied.

"Get them fastened tight an' correct," Millie said.

Shorty tried to speak. His words made no sense because of the pliers against his tongue. Nancy took her grip. She put a knee on Shorty's chest. Lips compressed, she twisted, pulling upward simultaneously.

Shorty said, "Gum, goo, go, gall," and then the pliers rose, the half-tooth glistening and with bloody roots.

Nancy held it up for Shorty's inspection. Shorty's tongue made explorations of the cavity. "Seems like a mite of root still is in the hole."

"That'll work out in time," Nancy said. "I need a drink."

"Here, Doctor Craig." Millie quickly handed her a bottle.

Shorty sat up. "I feel a mite better. Where's my bottle." Shorty spat blood on the floor. "Mop it up later."

Millie sat on Shorty's left. Nancy sat on his right on the bunk. Shorty said, very seriously, "Dee Bowden, dang your happy soul! Lord, how I miss you, boss. This is terrible, women."

"Worse than terrible," Nancy agreed.

"An' Dee's such a nice guy," Millie said.

Nancy began to cry. She put her dark head on Shorty's shoulder. Millie also began to weep. Shorty looked at the brunette head on his left shoulder, then at the blonde head resting on his right shoulder.

Crazy thoughts ran through his booze-drenched brain. He knew Dee had never shot and killed Craig. Dee would die before stooping as low as ambush. Dee was a man— his friend— No, more than a friend....

His buddy, Dee was. Always had been....

Who'd profit if Dee were killed? Who'd get his spread, his cattle? There'd be court business, of course. Did Dee have a will? No, he was sure Dee had made out no will.

Branch Craig had claimed Rafter V lost cattle to rustlers. Although he drank much, Craig had been an honest man, Shorty Messenger knew. If Craig had said he'd lost Rafter V stock to cowthieves, Craig had lost dogies to rustlers. And who were these cowthieves?

Shorty shook his head, tongue in empty tooth socket.

Nancy had quit weeping. She apparently had gone to sleep. Millie still sobbed. Millie now took another deep long drink of old Wolf Nelson's snake-bite cure.

"You're behin'," Shorty said. "Drink up, darlin'."

"I love Dee," Millie said.

"How come that?"

"He never makes any passes at me. He treats me like a lady. He's honest an' courteous an'—"

"An' he's my man," Nancy suddenly said.

Shorty said, "Figgered you was sleepin, Nancy darlin'?"

"I was but I ain't now. That's fightin' talk to me, Shorty."

"I'm sorry," Millie hurriedly said. "I want you as a friend, not an enemy, Nancy."

"I still don't cotton to such words," Nancy said.

Shorty said, "Let's be friends, beautiful ladies. No harsh words, no conflict, no fisticuffs.'

"Women don't hit," Millie corrected. "They use their fingernails. The pull hair. But mostly it's fingernails. I've seen saloon girls scarred for life with fingernail gouges."

"I've heard that said," Nancy said. "You know, I believe I'll go to sleep again."

"My shoulder— It's tired."

Despite Shorty's words, Nancy's brunette head came down again on his shoulder. "I'm goin' nap a bit, too," Millie said.

Her blonde head came down, penning Shorty between two lovely young females, but Shorty's mind was miles away, thinking about steers—and cows and calves— being hazed off Round Rock range.

One thing was certain: stolen beef had to find a ready market. And where was that market in this area?

Find the market, Shorty's drunken brain said.

Suddenly, Shorty felt powerfully sleepy. And that was odd for it was still forenoon. He yawned and said, "Dee Bowden, where the heck are you?" and without realizing it, he fell asleep sitting up.

He immediately began snoring.

Chapter Ten

Dee Bowden watches the posse sweep toward Diamond within a Diamond from high on the rock-strewn side of Moccasin Butte, two miles directly west of his home ranch in the badlands.

Hunkered there in the cold autumn wind, the cowpuncher realized he needed a number of things if he were to successfully remain a free man. First was a pair of good field glasses.

This was an area of limitless spaces that ran too far out for the naked human eye. You needed field glasses—or a telescope—to bring items closer to your vision.

He also needed blankets and a good sheepskin coat. This wind was cold and as fall progressed would grow colder.

And, above all, he needed a different horse.

He had picked a wind-broken saddler in Jim North's horse, for the horse had no bottom—it had been taken out of him through long runs and misuse. The bay was fast for a short distance but had no stamina for the long and tough runs Dee might be forced to hand him.

And upon a fast and tough horse depended the life of one Dee Bowden, Dee told himself as he watched the posse roll into the yard of Diamond inside a Diamond, his buildings hiding the horsemen from view.

He knew that Sheriff Isaac Watson was not fool enough to believe, he, Dee, would hide out on his own ranch. Watson was merely scouting to see if Shorty had seen his boss, Dee felt sure.

Dee grinned.

Watson would have no luck pumping Shorty for information. Shorty would pull off his *loco act* and Watson would get nothing but frustration. Dee had also seen Nancy ride south from Rafter V and turn off the wagon-road and ride west a short distance to enter his Diamond inside a Diamond.

Why had Nancy ridden seven miles south to visit the ranch of the man accused of bushwhacking her father? Certainly not because she cared for that man? Dee remembered the angry sessions with her after Branch Craig's death. Now, he shrugged.

Watson's riders did not remain long at his ranch. Soon they swept south again toward Round Rock, five miles distant. Two riders left the posse. One reined his horse up Moccasin Canyon, riding straight toward the hidden Dee, who recognized Jim North.

The other left the posse at the mouth of Devil's Canyon, south of Moccasin—the canyon wherein Wolf Nelson's hounds had found Byers' body. Despite the distance, Dee recognized that rider as Sheriff Watson.

The posse rode on, dust hanging.

Jim North rode to the Diamond inside a Diamond drift fence strung across the canyon, then drew rein and dismounted. Plainly he searched for certain horse-tracks on the dim trail.

Dee knew the man was an expert tracker, having spent his childhood with the Assiniboine tribe—his mother being a fullblooded Assiniboine squaw who had unwisely chosen a vagabond trapper.

And Jim North would surely know the tracks left by his own horse, Dee knew. But Dee had not ridden up the canyon. He had come across country to his high perch.

Within minutes, North was back in saddle. He turned his bronc and rode down the canyon toward the wagon-road twisting its dusty length south and north along the base of the igneous rimrock.

Once on level land, North put his horse at a faster pace, heading across the sagebrush and greasewood for Round Rock. Dee Bowden turned his attention on Sheriff Watson, some three miles south.

Sheriff Watson was in Devil's Canyon. Therefore Dee couldn't see the lawman. He turned his attention to a rider the posse had met and who had ridden on. That rider now was riding into Diamond inside a Diamond.

Dee scowled. Unless his range-trained eyes were wrong, that rider was none other than Millie, the Diamond Willow girl. And with Nancy Craig already at Diamond inside a Diamond—

Dee grinned. Shorty'd have his hands full of irate females, no doubt. Dee wanted desperately to ride into his home ranch but dared not, for Sheriff Watson might have stationed a deputy at the spread.

Dee had not been able to count the riders when they'd headed north to Diamond inside a Diamond. They had been too far away and closely bunched. The same took place when the posse rode back toward Round Rock.

To ride into his ranch might bring about arrest. Or death under roaring guns....if Sheriff Watson had stationed a guard—or guards.

He looked back at Jim North, now nearing the mouth of Devil's. North turned his horse west, entered the canyon—and disappeard. Dee shifted slightly, muscles tightening in one leg. He waited patiently.

Within a half hour, Watson and North rode out of Devil's Canyon. They turned broncs southeast toward Round Rock,.

Dee knew that this range held rifles and pistols against him. Five thousand dollars rode on his blonde head. Sheriff Isaac Watson was not taking a jailbreak and an ambush murder sitting home in his easy chair surrounded by his howling family of twelve youngsters.

Watson's job was at stake. You needed good wages to stow grub into fourteen healthy bellies, including his fat wife and himself. Watson would hunt him night and day.

Dee figured about every able-bodied male except Shorty on Round Rock grass would turn into a bounty-hunter. And he, Dee Bowden, would be the hunted. Dee felt frustration beat.

Where would he start? How could he clear his name and become the peaceful, hard-working citizen he'd been but a few days ago?

Although young, he realized men fought—and killed—mostly for money, with an occasional gunfight-of-honor occurring. These affairs of honor were in the minority, he knew.

Byers had held the secret. Now, Byers slept in a prairie grave. And Dee knew he had to start from scratch.

On this range, cattle were money. And Branch Craig had claimed he'd been losing cattle to rustlers.

Find the cowthieves, then? Was it that simple, that elemental? Dee saw Jim North and Sheriff Watson disappear behind the first of Round Rock's buildings. No riders or rigs were on the wagon-trail below stretching north from Round Rock and disappearing north of huge Rafter V as it twisted its way to the Montana border.

Dee mounted the bay and rode north. There he found a small canyon leading down to the plains below. He came out on level ground about two miles north of his Diamond inside a Diamond.

He knew tough Diamond inside a Diamond saddle-broncs grazed in this district. After beef roundup and after his cattle had been gathered on Greasewood Flats, the saddle-broncs had been turned loose onto open range.

Long circles during roundup had toughened the cayuses. He had ridden every bronc in the Diamond inside a Diamond remuda; therefore, he knew each horse's bottom and speed and stamina.

His fat cows grazed in bottoms and on side-hills. They were wild and when they saw him they stared, then wheeled and ran, tails up. They wanted nothing to do with a man on horseback.

They had recently been choused from grazing areas,

hammered over rumps with doubled lassos and bullwhips. They'd been driven into a milling bunch of bawling, snorting bovines.

Riders on tough Wyoming cayuses had circled them, holding them in a packed herd. If one of them had tried to break for freedom, an agile cowpony had headed him off, his rider beating him over the back with a bullwhip.

Dee drew rein in a clump of boxelder trees on a ridge. Below him was Dahl Springs. A man with a slip was cleaning out the spring.

Dee recognized Mack Weston. Weston wore hip-high rubber boots. He had two horses—Flip and Dan—hooked to the scraper.

Holding the slip by both handles, the hand pulled it into the muddy water, the team dutifully backing up. Then, the steel blade buried in black ooze, the cowboy drove the team ahead to dump the wet soil high on the opposite slope before returning for another slip-full of wet earth.

Dee remembered two women recently riding into Diamond inside a Diamond. He'd seen Shorty from a distance in the ranch-house yard. Shorty then was alone with two pretty females?

The lucky stiff, Dee thought.

Dee noticed Mack Weston's sheepskin coat thrown over the limb of a cottonwood a short distance from Dahl Springs. His eyes followed a trail down to that sheepskin, and he realized he could sneak down through brush, pull down the coat, and return to horse ... and Mack Weston, busy and muddy and slopping around in water, undoubtedly would not see him.

Mack didn't see him. Within ten minutes, Dee Bowden tied a heavy new windbreaker sheepskin coat behind his stolen Hamley saddle, leaving a baffled Mack Weston behind when time came to don his overcoat.

That evening at chuck a puzzled Mack Weston told a half-drunk Shorty Messenger of his coat's disappearance. "Danged thing must've jus' flewed away."

87

"Coats ain't got wings."

"That one must've had."

"You must've left it home. Have you looked?"

"All over. Nope, I wore it out to the Springs this mornin'. I hung it over a limb. An' when I looked later, it was gone."

"Who t'heck'd steal a coat?" Shorty felt gingerly of his jaw. "Swellin's goin' down. Thet woman is a good dentist."

"What in tarnation's you blabbin' about, Shorty?"

"I don't feel well."

"You smell like a whiskey vat. Another thing—that bay hoss Jones— He ain't grazin' aroun' Dahl Springs no more."

"Mebbe he never grazed there?"

"When I went out this mornin', there he was big as life with the other ponies, watchin' me to see I didn't lay a rope on him. When I druv the wagon home this sundown, he weren't there." ·

"I'm goin' turn in." Shorty stopped momentarily at the cook-shack door, filled coffee cup in hand. "Mebbe he drifted off somewhere to visit his grandmother?"

Shorty laughed sardonically and weaved his way toward the bunk house and his sougans. Back in the hills, Dee Bowden patted Jones on the shoulder. "You tough sonofagun," he said.

Jones grass-stained teeth snapped an inch from Dee's right ear. Dee leaped backwards just in time. Jones definitely did not cotton to humans.

Dee slapped Jones affectionately on the bony nose. He had his coat and his horse. Where would he get field-glasses?

Rafter V always had a hand in its linecamp on South Creek. And cowhands usually had field-glasses. He knew little Henry Halverson was usually stationed on South Creek to turn back cattle wanting to drift north and off of Rafter V range.

Henry was about sixty and very near sighted. Dee

spent a miserable night back in the badlands trying to cover himself with Mack Weston's sheepskin coat—and there was definitely more Dee Bowden than there was sheepskin.

He dared not light a campfire. A fire might be seen. A bounty-hunter might sneak in and— Daylight came in with a cold wind.

He built a horsehair snare and caught a young cottontail. Taking a chance, he lit a very small fire on the slope of a brush-covered butte where he could see miles and miles in all directions.

He used very dry greasewood twigs. They made little—if any—tell-tale smoke. He broiled the tender flesh on a stick. He had no salt but the meal was one of the most delicious he'd ever eaten, he was that famished.

Inner man fed, he drank from a spring oozing out of solid rock, and decided to get his necessary field glasses. Accordingly, he left the badlands and rode northeast, heading for South Creek which, despite its name, was the northern limit of Rafter V's vast range.

Seven o'clock found him watching the South Creek linecamp, sitting Jones in high buckbrush on the hill to the east. Smoke came from the log cabin's stovepipe chimney. Henry Halverson was evidently cooking breakfast.

Dee considered dismounting and barging in on the cowpuncher but discarded that, for Henry was rather well-known for his rapid gun-play—and Dee felt sure the cowboy would be packing his six-shooter, even while standing before the wood-burning cookstove.

Dee rode Jones downslope and sat his saddle hidden by brush, watching the cabin's door. Soon a man came out. And that line-rider was definitely not small Henry Halverson.

This man was short, wide-shouldered, tough-looking. Dee recognized Jupp Gardiner, one of Rafter V's toughest riders—and Dee Bowden had definitely no desire to tangle with Gardiner.

Gardiner bowlegged his way to the brush-barn, entered. Dee heard him cursing. He also heard a boot thud into flesh. Gardiner had kicked a saddler in the belly. Dee knew Gardiner was a tough hand with a horse, also.

Gardiner left the makeshift barn, leading a black stud he'd saddled in the shed. He tied his lunch-bucket onto the saddle and swung up, the black humping his back and wanting to buck.

Gardiner was a crack bronc-stomper. He'd won three bronc riding firsts in the railroad rodeo—saddle-bronc riding, bareback bronc riding and curcingle bronc stomping.

"Wanna buck, huh? Okay, black hoss, hop to it!"

Gardiner anchored his gross body deep between fork and cantle, grinning happily. His star-roweled Kelly spurs rose, hesitated—then whammed down, raking the black's muscle-bunched shoulders.

The black broke immediately into pitching. Head down, forelegs stiff, he slammed into it, Gardiner easily riding him, spurs raking fore and aft in best stampede fashion.

Then, something happened to Jupp Gardiner. One moment, he was solid in saddle; the next, he flew unconscious to land on his belly in the dust.

The black bucked on, empty stirrups flapping. Immediately a rider whammed in, catching the black's reins. With one mighty heave, that rider pulled up the bucking horse's head—and when a bronc's head is up, he can't buck.

Jupp Gardiner still lay motionless.

Dee hurriedly dismounted. He tore the lunch-pail and field-glasses from behind the black's cantle. Fear tore at him. Had he slugged Gardiner too hard? Had he accidentally killed the bronc-stomper?

He shot a hurried glance toward the prone man as he swung up on Jones, stolen articles in hand. Relief flooded him when he saw Gardiner's hands clawing gravel.

Dee spurred out of the yard. High buckbrush claimed him. He rode hard to the west. About a hundred yards from the line-camp he had to cross a clearing.

Suddenly, his cantle behind him jerked hard. He glanced back, surprised. A man stood in the cabin's doorway, pistol raised. Dee realized a bullet had slapped into the back of his saddle.

Apparently another rider had been also stationed at Dahl Springs? Riding twisted in saddle. Dee's .45 lifted. He shot over the man and not at him. His hastily-flung bullets drove the man back into the cabin.

Dee hadn't recognized the pistolman. He was sure he had not been Jupp Gardiner. The pistolman had looked tall and slim, not heavy-set and stolid with wide shoulders.

Who had the man been? A drifter, maybe? A grubline rider who'd spent the night in the cabin before drifting on?

Curiosity held Dee. He also wanted to see if Jupp Gardiner had got to this feet. Accordingly, he ground-tied Jones in a clump of pine trees and, rifle in hand, he returned to the cabin on foot.

He arrived just in time to see the tall man swing into saddle on a gray horse bearing a brand alien to Dee, the N Bar S. The man spurred the horse out of the yard, pointing the beast south.

Dee looked at Gardiner. He was stirring and mumbling something. He grinned. This drifter was wasting no time shaking out of this line-camp. He didn't want Gardiner to come to and accuse him of slugging him, evidently?

The drifter fell from sight in a coulee. Jupp Gardiner got shakily afoot, staring wildly about.

His gaze fell on his old Stetson, a few feet distant. He wobbled toward the hat, almost falling as he bent to retrieve it.

He carefully re-creased the battered hat. Then he hollered, "Drifter, damn you! Where are you?"

Of course, he got no answer. He stared at his horse, standing with trailing reins.

"What the heck—? My lunch pail's gone! So are my field glasses! Hey, drifter!"

Again, no answer.

Dee grinned in his concealment. Jupp Gardiner was not hurt. He had proved one thing—he had the right touch on his gun-barrel when he slugged a man.

"Damn you, drifter, come outa that cabin!"

Jupp Gardiner turned on uncertain boots. He stared at the cabin's gaping door. Evidently his mind still had some cobwebs. Dee realized the man still was not thinking straight. Common sense should have told Gardiner that if the drifter had slugged him the drifter by now would be long gone.

Gardiner pushed back his hat. Grimy fingers felt of his head. "Gotta big bump there. Thet drifter— He must've rid in on his cayuse an' slugged me but for why?"

Dee's grin widened. Gardiner had the habit of talking to himself, a trait men alone for long periods of time acquired.

Gardiner entered the cabin, legs steadier now. He came out with a perplexed look on his face. He peered into the barn. The look grew.

"Damn' drifter's done went! He packed a lunch to take with him— It was on the table. It's gone. He took it. He also stole my lunch. An' my field-glasses— Hell, he packed glasses. An' he stole mine? A man can only see through one pair of field-glasses at a time, too!"

Dee had heard enough. Gardiner had not glimpsed him ride in from behind, pistol raised.

Dee slipped back into the brush. The last words he heard Gardiner say were, "Awful headache I got, bronc."

Dee grinned.

Chapter Eleven

Ten o'clock the next morning Shorty Messenger sat with his back against a diamond-willow fence-post in the Moccasin Canyon drift fence and with a long sliver of wood teased an ant determined to crawl past the cowboy, something Shorty was equally determined would not happen.

Moccasin Canyon was some fifty feet wide at this point. The fence consisted of six barbwire strands. The bottom of the canyon consisted of sand and boulders showing hoof marks of cattle, horses and deer.

The deer, of course, had leaped the fence but the cows and horses had been turned back. Shorty breathed deeply, his hangover completely gone against a night of solid sleep.

Suddenly he said, "Sheriff Isaac Watson, ride forth!"

His words rang up the canyon's brush-thick walls. Had an onlooker been present he would have thought the cowpuncher completely loco for calling out to a man who apparently was not in hearing range.

But Shorty Messenger was not loco. And Sheriff Isaac Watson was in hearing range although the lawman did not answer immediately so Shorty said in a louder voice, "Sheriff, comest thou out of the brush on Moccasin Canyon's south slope."

The brush made rattling sounds. A small boulder rolled down, evidently loosened by some moving object.

The boulder came to a rest on the canyon's sandy bottom.

Sheriff Isaac Watson and horse soon slid down the slope to land on the bottom, the lawman leading his black mare. Watson's homely face bore a smile designating both anger and embarrassment.

"How long have you knowed I was hidin' up there, Shorty?"

"About two hours. I bin settin' here about a hour. I've done turned back eight ants to this moment but this one is the most stubborn of all, the little tyke."

"How come you see me ride intuh this canyon?"

"I was settin' up on the north ridge. Saw you come out from town. Then when you turned west into Moccasin I come down to play with these ants."

Sheriff Watson winced. "Where's your bronc?"

"Yonder. Hid in boulders on the north ridge. Now this little tike of an ant—"

"I figger you aimed to meet Dee Bowden here, Shorty."

Shorty looked up in surprise. "Meet Dee—? Here—? Why here, sher'ff? Why not somewhere else?"

Sheriff Watson sighed deeply. "I like you, Messenger. I've knowed you since you was a baby. Sometimes I feel like I'm allowin' sentiment to make me shirk my duty, though."

Shorty's eyes were without emotion. "Now kin you explain thet to me, sher'ff? In simple, everyday words?"

"I know no other words. I'm danged sure you jerked my jail apart with a wagon team an' a log chain. Young Sonny Wilkinson yesterday done found a log chain throwed under the Merc store-room."

"He's lucky. Now, with a stout horse, he can pull town cows outa the crick bog. Them danged cows—"

"Shorty, I believe I'll have to throw you in jail."

Shorty nodded. "Have you got the jail patched up ag'in, sher'ff?"

"They're cementin' in the bars today. By the time you an' me reach town, the calaboose will be ready."

Shorty got to his feet. "Somebody to cook for me there?"

"Your meals will come from the Star Cafe. All prisoners get meals from the Star."

"At county expense?"

"Yeah, at county expense. Why the tarnation you so interested in the jail-grub?"

"Me an' Mack Weston's alone at Diamond. Thet Dee Bowden— Too cheap to hire a cook. So me an' Mack have to take turns at thet danged woodburner an'— One thing I hate more than hard drink an' that is cookin', sher'ff."

"You want to go to jail so's you'd get some cooked meals?"

Shorty snapped his stick in two. "That's the deal, Mr. Watson. I'm ready to go when you're ready."

The sheriff studied the waddy's wide, homely face. This fool was in earnest! Sheriff Watson felt both angry and stupid. He was angry because, in stupidity, he had fallen into Shorty Messenger's verbal trap.

"Go to hell," the sheriff said.

Without another word, he swung onto his black mare, wheeled her about, and loped down the canyon, the mare's steel-shod hoofs throwing back sand. The corner came in and hid him.

Shorty got down on his knees. He laughed and beat the sand with doubled hands, praying that somewhere up on some butte Dee Bowden watched through field glasses or a telescope—for by now surely Dee had appropriated either or both of these instruments.

Laughter over, he climbed the brushy north slope of Moccasin Canyon to where his iron-gray gelding stood hip-humped in the high sandstones out of the chilly fall Wyoming wind.

Shorty pulled a big red silk bandana from a hip pocket and did a Sioux war dance on a level area, waving the bandana over his stetson to tell a watching Dee that danger was around and he could not meet him as they had agreed.

This done, he looked south toward Round Rock. Sheriff Isaac Watson was not in sight on the wagon road or on the flat lands stretching out in all directions many feet below.

Shorty smiled. Watson had reined west. Again, he was threading another gulch lifting into the badlands. This time Watson would leave his bronc behind. And work his way on foot again into Moccasin Canyon?

Well, Shorty wouldn't be in Moccasin when the lawman arrived, Shorty told himself as he put his bronc down the north slope, thus putting a high hill between himself and the sheriff.

Shorty rode north, close to the rimrock's base. Thus he was hidden from Sheriff Watson's view. Within an hour, he was on Diamond's northern limits.

He searched for a four-year-old brockle-faced cow—a marker. This was the cow Craig had accused Dee Bowden of stealing, that day in the Diamond Willow when both had gone for guns—and had not Sheriff Watson grabbed Craig's gunarm, Dee might have been killed.

Dee had meant to ship the cow but the eastern cow-buyer had turned her down. Not enough fat on her ribs, the buyer had said.

The cow had been driven back to Diamond inside a Diamond range. She usually grazed three miles away from the home ranch, southeast around Wilson's Springs.

Shorty had ridden that area early this morning. The marker had been missing. He had swung out, riding circle. He had not found the cow.

Maybe the ornery critter had strayed north? That hardly seemed possible. Cows were like humans. A cow grazed in a certain confined area, seldom wandering beyond these limits unless driven. A human also ranged within established borders.

Shorty knew coyotes and pumas also had definite limits to their hunting areas. Should they stray beyond these limits they'd move into the hunting area of another wilding and fur would fly.

Shorty came to the Round Rock wagon-road. He drew rein and watched a fastly-moving rider approach. The rider came closer. Shorty recognized Jupp Gardiner, a Rafter V hand. "Which devil is chasin' you, Jupp?"

"Ridin' into Roun' Rock to tell Sheriff Watson that this mornin' a drifter I fed stole my field glasses. An' if'n I catch thet drifter in town I'll—"

"A man's gotta be right keerful who he takes in this time of the year," Shorty said. "You'll fin' Sher'ff Watson in Moccasin Canyon."

"Moccasin Canyon? What's he doin' there?"

"Watchin' for Dee Bowden. He seems to think Dee would meet me in Moccasin. I don't think he'll pay much heed to your complaint, though."

"Why not?"

"He's up to his nick in bigger troubles. Who's boss on Rafter V now? The purty female?"

"Right now she is."

"What'd you mean by right now, Jupp?"

Jupp explained. Nancy would ramrod Rafter V until school started. "She still aims to teach them wild kids, I hear. When she moves into Round Rock to live in the teacher's quarters ahind the school I understand Bat Morgan will be ramrod completely."

Bat Morgan was now range-boss, a job he held for years under Branch Craig.

"Who's bossin' Diamon' now that Bowden is on the run?" Jupp Gardiner asked.

"Me."

Gardiner took off his hat and bowed in saddle. "Glad to meet you, High Mucky Muck."

"You got a clump on your haid, Jupp. How come?"

Angrily, Gardiner restored his Stetson. He told about the incident at line-camp.

Shorty said, "Then you ain't sure whether the drifter rid in an' slugged you for your lunch an' your glasses?"

"Somebody rode in, but I never saw hide or hair of him. Come in from the back when I was rakin' the hell outa that cayuse."

"Mebbe the cayuse done throwed you?"

Immediately, Jupp Gardiner's dander was up. "Thet thing throw me—? Hell, he could buck from here to Christmas an'— What're you doin' ridin' this neck of the timber?"

Shorty told about the four-year-old brockle-faced roan cow. "You see the critter about, Jupp?"

Gardiner shook his head. "Not hide nor hair of her, Shorty. I know thet critter, too. She's the one Branch accused Bowden of rebrandin' that day in the Diamon' Willow, ain't she?"

"That's her, Jupp."

"She ain't hereabouts, Shorty. I've rid this grass from the Belly Down Hills to the Rimrock an' I'd've seen her if she was aroun'. Marker, too, ain't she?"

"That she is." Shorty shifted in stirrups. "You danged sure Rafter's been rustled?"

"That's what Craig said. When we hit beef roundup a few weeks back Branch's tally came in way short."

"How many head?"

"Aroun' a thousan' head, if not more. Branch kept tally alone at first. He couldn't believe his count so he had Bat Morgan keep a separate tally, an' Bat's count was a hundred odd head more gone than even Branch's."

Shorty whistled. "Lotta dogies."

"You missed any?"

"Dee said a few were short, but they might've drifted. But with this brockle-face gone—"

"I'll keep my eyes open an' ears peeled back. If'n I see her, I'll report back. Where'll you be?"

"Sher'ff says I should be behin' bars. If'n not in the town jail somewhere aroun' Diamon' inside a Diamon'."

"You an' thet sher'ff," Gardiner said. "Always scrappin'. Heck, no use me reportin' such a small theft to such a busy lawman. Like you say, Watson's got both hands filled with findin' your boss."

"That he has."

Gardiner neckreined his sweaty bronc around. "I ain't got much to do, an' what I've got kin wait. I'll help you hunt."

"I'd be grateful fer your company, Jupp."

"She might be northwest along the rimrock. Water an' grass is scarce this time of the year. A bit more bluestem grows in that area along the springs there."

Shorty nodded. "Or mebbe northeast along Smuthers' Bog. Water an' bluestem a mite more there, too."

"Which way do we ride, Shorty?"

"Let's flip a coin. You got any money?"

Gardiner dug. "Four bits, that's all. Pay day ain't far off, though. What' you take?"

"Tails."

Gardiner tossed up the coin. Short decided he not try to contact Dee today. Sheriff Watson was too much in attendance. Besides, what did he have to tell Dee that would help Dee's cause?

Not a thing. Of course, he could tell Dee about a ranch-owner—female—and a saloon-girl and four bottles of old Wolf Nelson's snakebite cure. Yes, and how he'd had a tooth pulled.

His tongue sought the tooth's empty socket. There still was that piece of bone to get rid of. His tongue played with it.

The coin landed. "Tails," Gardiner said. "You win."

Shorty seemed suddenly far away. He sat saddle with an idle grin on his homely face.

Where was his pal, Dee? Had Dee slugged Jupp? And stolen Jupp's field-glasses? And lunch?

Dee needed field-glasses. Shorty had a sudden hunch that his boss had been Jupp Gardiner's unseen assailant. Shorty grinned.

"You win," Gardiner repeated.

Shorty Messenger came back to earth. "I was born with a silver spoon in my mouth," he said.

They rode northeast.

Chapter Twelve

Outside the ever-present Wyoming prairie-wind whistled in the eaves of Banker John Hendricks' quarters behind his bank. Inside the Franklin coal-burner was red with fiery Wyoming lignite.

John Hendricks put his boot on a chair as he strapped down his star-rowled Garcia spur. "Golden Gulch," he said slowly. "Long ride, Mark."

Mark Stratton removed his cigar. "I've ridden it," he said dryly. "Where in the hell, John, is that Craig money?"

Spur strap adjusted, Hendricks stood up. A green silk bandana was tied around his head under his flat-brimmed Stetson to keep his ears warm. A sheepskin coat covered his narrow shoulders.

Heavily-furred angora chaps graced his legs.

"Don't ask me," he said. He picked up his .25-20 rifle, jacked the lever down; a cartridge lifted, fell to the floor. He squinted into the barrel, making sure a new cartridge had slid into the bore.

"It has to be in Devil's Canyon," Stratton said.

Hendricks crammed the thrown-out cartridge into the rifle's magazine. He set the trigger on safety.

"We roasted an' toasted Byers," the banker said, "an' he never tol' us where he'd hid the money. Took us to where he *said he'd hid it* but the ground was open and if it had been there, it was gone."

"He lied."

Hendricks shrugged. "He stuck to his lie, if lying he was. You got to give the bastard credit for that."

Stratton took a drink from the bottle on the table. "And then that stinkin' ol' Wolf Nelson had to come along—with his damn' hounds." He put the bottle back on the table. "I reckon I'll ride out to thet damn' canyon an' look aroun' again."

"You'll find nothing."

Stratton got to his feet. "Wolf Nelson's got Craig's money. Byers buried it. Nelson's hounds smelled it. Nelson dug it out."

Hendricks emptied a box of .25-20 cartridges into his overcoat pocket. The open sheepskin coat showed a broad, cartridge-heavy gunbelt circled his slim waist. His black-handled .45 Colt hung on his right hip.

Hendricks straightened. Suddenly, he laughed—low, sardonically. Stratton glanced at the banker. "What's so damned funny?"

"Us."

"I don't get you."

"We bust out of that Texas pen. Old Huntsville pen, itself—toughest pen in the west."

Stratton glanced significantly toward the closed door leading to the bank proper.

"Old Sig Livingston's at his desk at the far end. On top of that, he's hard hearing. He'll run the bank while I ride to Golden Gulch. Well, Cy Zachary—our old stir-mate— he gets out six months ahead of our prison break."

"No use recitin' our miseries." Stratton suddenly opened the back door. He peered out and saw only the empty alley with its garbage cans.

"You're getting edgy," Hendricks said.

"We made a mistake takin' Byers north with us when we all decided to pull north into Canada—an' when Cy got word to us a fortune was waitin' for us here on this range."

"Right you are there," Hendricks agreed. "One of us should have ambushed Craig and got his money. But one

101

good thing came out of it. We got that Bowden on the run—all the blame on him—"

"Wonder where Bowden is?"

Hendricks pulled on sheepskin lined mittens. "Be a might cold up close to the Tetons. I don't know where he is but he won't be around long, you can bet on that."

"Five thousand dollars, dead or alive."

Stratton sat down again. "That should soon finish him. Winter's comin' on. Lot of cowpunchs laid off. They'll head out, mebbe, and hunt Bowden? Too bad we didn't get a chance to kill him out on the prairie the night we all rode out—the night Craig got killed."

"He never gave us a chance. Had he offered a little resistance, I'd have shot him down."

Stratton looked up at the banker, eyes heavy. "You suppose anybody here is suspicious of us, John?"

Hendricks laughed. "Would they have any reason to be?"

Stratton got to his boots again, gunbelt creaking. "I reckon not. Saloon-owner an' banker, honest citizens. Wonder if the boys have stolen any of Bowden's stock while Bowden has been runnin'?"

"Cy Zachary misses no bets. I'll be back day after tomorrow, maybe. If not, add a day, friend."

"I'll hold down the fort. Where'd you tell your clerk you was headin'?"

"South. Bankers' meeting, Buffalo Bend."

Banker John Hendricks pulled up his rifle and left, cold air whipping in as the door opened and closed. Stratton touched a sulphur to his cigar. Unrest pulled in the big saloon-keeper.

He paced the small room, boots heavy on the pine floor. He remembered an old Round Rock citizen hanging dead, back against the door of his upstairs Diamond Willow quarters.

A rope had run upward from Happy Jayson's thin neck. It had gone over the top of the door and down to be tied to the doorknob. When the chair had been pulled out, Jayson had fallen three feet—and you could hear his neck snap with a sharp crack.

Stratton paced, grinning. Easy hanging. Knockout drops in coffee down below in the Diamond Willow. "Gettin' sleepy. Guess I'll go upstairs an' take a nap. Good to have met you, stranger."

Old Happy had hit the rope's end, mouth sagging open.

Stratton stopped, listening. The wind, as usual, howling in eaves—always the damned wind. Only time it went down for a few minutes was at sunup and sundown. Then the mosquitoes buzzed in by the thousands.

He heard a horse lope past in the alley. Stratton pushed the dirty curtain slightly aside and caught a glimpse of John Hendricks's bronc turning the corner.

Hendricks rode down Main Street, nodding and lifting a hand to his customers, the genial good-natured banker. "Where to, John?" called a man in front of the Merc and Hendricks hollered back, "Buffalo Bend. Conflab there."

"Be a long cold ride, John."

"Got to go, Bill."

Hendricks found the wagon-trail leading south. He rode along it for five miles until he came to Deming's ranch. Here he had a cup of hot coffee and a brief conversation with Tom Deming, the iron's owner.

"Buffalo Bend," Hendricks said.

He rode on. A mile south, he left the wagon-trail, reining west toward a canyon running down from the rimrock, half a mile away. Two hundred yards off the trail, he reined-up in a motte of chokecherry trees and looked back at the wagon-trail, now below him.

No rigs or riders were in sight. His ruse had been successful. All thought he was riding south. He found the canyon, threaded up it to come out on a high, windswept mesa.

The mesa consisted mostly of solid rock outcroppings.

103

Here and there grew sagebrush almost as high as his saddle. Wind whipped harder here, chilling his ears through his bandana.

The banker put his blue-roan stud at a long trail lope that was easy on rider and on horse. He followed no trail, for there was none. The stud's steel shod hoofs echoed occasionally as he crossed igneous areas.

John Hendricks rode deep in Miles City saddle, Hyer boots anchored in oxbow stirrups, head pulled down into the sheepskin collar of his overcoat, more or less letting his stud pick his own way.

The horse had apparently traveled this area before. He pointed himself northwest. Hendricks rode with loose reins, trusting his mount. Occasionally he reared his head and looked at his surroundings.

And what he saw definitely did not please him. East he could just catch the far edge of Round Rock basin with its leafless trees along Medicine River. South was wastelands, west more of the same.

North was as foreboding as south and west. Not enough grass grew here even during wet seasons to keep a goat. Few jackrabbits were in existence. Jackrabbits were too smart. They liked the green areas in the basin along Beaver and Round Rock creeks.

What little life that existed lived around springs back in the draws, and these life-giving water-holes were few and far between. Occasionally Hendricks pulled the stud down to a fast running-walk.

The stud played with the port on his spade bit. He chewed and snorted as though seeking a diversion during the long pull. Hendricks glanced east. Here Devil's Canyon rose and petered out, losing its lift and identity on the flinty table-top.

A few miles further, and he came to the uplift and end of Moccasin Canyon. He caught the stinking odor of dead flesh. The cow was a Diamond within a Diamond critter, and had been dead some days.

The wind howled in from the west. Hendricks rode

west of the dead cow to escape its stink. He understood what had happened. Diamond inside the Diamond cattle had wandered up Moccasin before Dee Bowden had run his drift-fence across the canyon's western end.

The cow had become locked in on this mesa. She had died from starvation and lack of water.

He glanced west. Three miles away high Moccasin Butte reared its flat-topped hugeness upward into the cloudless Wyoming sky, its steep slopes marked by huge sandstone boulders and scraggly juniper trees.

Hendricks looked back northwest. He rode on. He did not know that Dee Bowden watched him from the west flank of Moccasin Butte.

Dee's stolen field glasses showed the banker clearly. Dee knew for sure the rider was John Hendricks because he recognized the blue-roan stud. Jupp Gardiner had carried good field-glasses. They were more powerful than Dee's, down home on his Beaver Creek spread.

The glasses had been fixed on Moccasin Canyon when Shorty Messenger had ridden up the gulch's depths an hour ago. They had also picked out Sheriff Isaac Watson and his black mare in hiding on Moccasin Canyon's south slope.

He'd seen Shorty and the lawman conflabing. Then the sheriff had ridden down the canyon, and Shorty had met Jupp Gardiner down on the basin's floor. Gardiner and Shorty had then ridden northeast and out of sight.

Dee had smiled as he had watched Sheriff Isaac Watson work his way back into Moccasin. Evidently Watson had figured correctly that he and Shorty had had a deal to meet in Moccasin?

But such a meeting, with Watson lurking in the wings, of course could not be held. Therefore Dee Bowden had worked his way up Moccasin Butte, leading his Jones horse.

He was a man with a small fortune resting on his head. Hunted men did not ride coulees or canyons. They rode high ridges. From a high point they could see the land around them. Enemies could be quickly located.

Dee studied Hendricks carefully. Where was the banker going? There was no close town situated northwest. The nearest burg, he had heard, was the gold boom camp, Golden Gulch.

He'd never been in Golden Gulch. He'd had no call to ride the eighty odd miles to the booming placer-gold area. He'd heard, though, that the free gold had lured thousands into the Teton area.

Dee came to the conclusion that business pulled Hendricks the direction of Golden Gulch. What other than a dollar would get a banker into saddle on a day as raw and chilly as this?

Or was Hendricks out hunting one Dee Bowden in hopes of winning the five thousand bucks on Bowden's head? Dee smiled at that assumption. Then another thought struck the young racher.

Had Hendricks been victim of a false rumor saying that he, Dee, had ridden into Golden Gulch? And did Hendricks now ride northwest to check that rumor?

Dee guessed many rumors of his whereabouts floated around Round Rock at this moment. One thing was sure, though—Hendricks did not search for him on this range for had the banker been looking for him Hendricks would not ride so openly.

Hendricks would sneak through the high brush, .25-20 in hand.

Dee's stolen glances followed the banker northwest until Hendricks and roan stud dropped from sight. Should he trail Hendricks?

Dee realized trailing would be impractical. Hendricks might glimpse him and lift his rifle from saddle-boot, for here there was very little foliage to conceal a rider as he rode northwest.

Dee looked at the sky. Days were getting shorter. Nightfall was not far off. Where would he spend the night?

Would he ride down into the basin, there to sneak into

106

some unoccupied Rafter V linecamp? Linecamps had beds and blankets in addition to grub. He needed both.

He rubbed his whiskery jaw. Dollars to doughnuts that every single linecamp in Round Rock basin was being watched. Each had a bounty-hunter hidden close, rifle at the ready were Dee Bowden to ride in.

No, not that....

Another chilly Wyoming fall night faced him. Another meal of cottontail cooked over a small smokeless fire on a stick.

This night, though, he did not eat rabbit. His snares caught a fat sagehen. The sagehen had dark brown flesh from eating sage. The rooster must have been about ten years old for his flesh was like rubber even when thoroughly cooked.

Dee chewed hard, wondering how old a sagehen grew to be. He gulped down the sagebrush-smelling flesh. He looked at the bone he held. Had he a dog, the dog would have had that bone.

But he had no dog.

He spent a chilly night. He walked part of the night to keep warm. Morning came with a cold sun creeping up. Anger filled the rancher. With this anger was frustration.

Today he'd contact Shorty Messenger, or die trying, for Shorty might have some information vital to his cause.

He tightened his Hamley's cinch. Jones, who'd been on lasso-picket, tried to bite him, stained teeth snapping. Dee looked at the bullet hole in the Hamley's cantle.

The bullet had not penetrated the cantle. The saddle-tree was bullhide wrapped three times for Jim North roped heavy stock—horses—and he needed an extra stout saddle-tree.

Dee swung into the Hamley, pointing Jones east toward the rimrock's ledge. Dawn was past. Therefore again the wind howled.

And that wind was very cold.

Chapter Thirteen

Mark Stratton did not ride into Devil's Canyon that day. Upon returning to his saloon, he got into a poker game. The game broke up around midnight. His luck was bad. He lost around a hundred dollars.

While playing, he kept his ears open. Gossip ran back and forth. Dee Bowden had left the country for good. Dee had been seen north of Rafter V. He'd been sighted far east.

Stratton scowled.

Dee had been seen in Blasted Stone. On hearing this rumor, Mark Stratton pricked up his ears. Blasted Stone was thirty miles straight north. Golden Gulch lay about thirty-five miles northwest of Blasted Stone.

He didn't like the idea of Dee being close to Golden Gulch. "I fade out," he had said. "Luck's muddy tonight, gentlemen."

"Dee was seen by a Deming cowboy way down south," a Rafter V cowboy said. "I know Mangano. When Mangano says he saw Dee way down south, Mangano seen him. Dee couldn't have been in Blasted Stone."

Mark Stratton dealt.

He awakened before dawn. His quarters were ice-cold. He threw paper and wood into the potbellied stove. He fried an egg on top of the heater in a thick castiron skillet. His coffee was already boiling.

He rode out on his blazed-faced sorrel gelding before

daylight had really arrived. His aim was to catch old Wolf Nelson in bed, for then the coyote-hunter might be sober.

The minute his eyes came open, Wolf reached out for his bottle, Stratton had been told. Stratton loped through the semi-darkness, sorrel following the wagon-trail running north.

Within minutes, he dismounted in front of Wolf's closed door, sixshooter in hand. He did not knock. He strode to the plank door. His right boot went out hard.

The door flew in.

Stench rolled from the cabin. Mingled with the stink of unwashed premises and an unwashed body was the odor of whiskey.

Stratton strode inside. He saw he had arrived too late. Old Wolf Nelson sat on the edge of his filthy bunk.

Dirty long-handled underwear covered his gaunt body. His old clothes lay in a heap on the unswept dirt floor.

His right hand clutched a whiskey bottle. He was in the act of lowering the bottle when Mark Stratton had barged in.

"What'd you want, *saloon keeper?*"

Stratton loathed being called a *saloon keeper*. The name was an insult. It was like calling a legitimate gambler a *tinhorn*. Stratton knew this old recluse had deliberately insulted him.

"How many shots you had this mornin'?"

Old Wolf raised the bottle again. Fiery alcohol tumbled down his throat, making his wizened Adam's Apple bob. He drained the bottle halfway down before Stratton stepped forward and batted it from the wolfer's grip.

The bottle sailed to one side, jetting whiskey. It landed on the dirt floor. It rolled but it didn't break.

Old Wolf lowered his empty hand, anger flaring in dull blue eyes. "You big son-of-a—"

He never completed the word. Stratton's big palm slapped the lean, whiskery cheek. Old Wolf glared up at

109

the saloon-man. "What'd you want?"

"The money."

"What money?"

"The money you stole off Byers. The money you dug up in Devil's Canyon."

"Byers? Where'd he get any money? He was just a simple cowpuncher, forty per month an' found."

"You know damn' well where Byers got that money! An' you know damn' well where that money is right now!"

A red tongue wet cracked lips. "I don't understan' why you an' thet banker claims I kilt Byers to get Craig's money."

"Where's that money, Nelson?"

Old Wolf looked at the bottle Stratton had knocked from his hand. It lay on its side. It still had a few snorts left, he quickly noticed.

Old Wolf was a drunk, yes—but not a fool. He knew that if Stratton or Hendricks got their hands on the stolen Craig money he was a dead wolfer. They'd kill him to silence him.

There was, he reasoned, only one way he could stay alive. That was to keep the stolen money out of the hands of the banker and saloon-keeper.

He wet his lips again. "Will you get me my bottle, Mr. Stratton?"

Stratton laughed. "That's better. Much better. Mr. Stratton. . . . Call me a saloon keeper again and I'll kick your damned teeth out!"

Old Wolf's laugh showed toothless gums. "Ain't got a tooth in my head, Mr. Stratton. They all rotted and fell out an'—"

"I'm not interested in rotten teeth, Nelson. I'm interested in Branch Craig's fortune."

The bottle rose. Raw moonshine gurgled down a leathery throat. Stratton watched with admiration.

This old wolfer could really stand liquid flame. You had to take your Stetson off to his drinking ability.

Stratton knew that that much of this wild firewater

110

would soon send him reeling, dead drunk and out on his boots. And he'd drunk many a stout man under the table.

Finally, the bottle came down . . . empty.

"Want me to take you to Devil's an' show you, Mr. Stratton?"

"That's why I'm here."

"Now mind this, Mr. Stratton. I gotta get a part of thet money."

"You get one-third, like Mr. Hendricks said the other day."

"Will yuh put thet in writin'?"

Stratton studied the whiskery face. "Do you think I'm completely crazy, Nelson? Stolen money . . . an' a written contract? You need another drink, wolfer."

"Thet I do. Glad you reminded me." Wolf Nelson dropped to his knees and reached under his bed.

Stratton's big .45 lifted. "Take it easy, Nelson. You come outa there with a rifle or pistol, an' I'm shootin' you right in the back of your dirty head!"

Wolf Nelson peered up. "What if I come out with a shotgun?"

"Don't get funny," Stratton warned.

Nelson said, "Okay, my arm is comin' out. What does thet look like? Neck of a bottle or a firearm?"

"Bottle."

A few minutes later, the pair rode toward Devil's Canyon, a shovel tied over the back of Stratton's hand-carved, ornate Denver saddle—for old Wolf Nelson rode bareback on his dun mule, one bottle in hand beside his reins and another protruding, neck up, from under his old cotton shirt.

Stratton wore a long sheepskin coat. Old Wolf wore only his thin shirt with fortification consisting of rotgut inside his scrawny body.

"I miss my houn's," Wolf Nelson said. "Always they go with me. Like leavin' my right han' at home."

"Those hounds have caused me too much trouble now."

111

"I don't figger out what you mean, Mr. Stratton."

"Think about it," Stratton growled.

The saloon man's miserable mood had increased. The cold wind, for one thing—this obstinate, stinking old bastard, for another. And losing money in a poker game with ignorant cowpokes who most couldn't even write their own names—

"Why for you pack that short-handled spade?" old Wolf asked.

"You're goin' do some diggin'. An' you better dig in the right place or else— Needs I say more, you stinkin' ol' goat?"

"No more, Mr. Stratton."

They reined broncs west, entering Devil's Canyon. Here the wind whistled even louder and stronger, for the canyon acted as a funnel—and the wind came from directly west.

"Be a bad, bad winter," old Wolf said. "I kin feel it in my bones."

"You'll be warm soon enough. Shovelin' will heat you up."

Old Wolf drank, handed the bottle to Stratton, who took a short swig. Stratton liked the whiskey's taste. They were right. Old Wolf Nelson moonshined better whiskey than that he imported for his saloon.

Neither knew that Dee Bowden, high on the mesa, had seen the pair ride out of Wolf Nelson's yard, his field-glasses identifying each rider despite the distance.

Dee pulled in Jones and frowned thoughtfully. Why had Mark Stratton ridden this cold morning to old Wolf Nelson's shack? And where were the saloon-man and the coyote-hunter going?

Dee watched the pair turn up Devil's Canyon and go out of sight. Something was going on here, he realized—for had not Hank Byers' burned body been found by old Wolf's hounds in Devil's Canyon?

And the two drifters Hank Byers had said he'd seen—

They had ridden up Devil's, according to Byers. Dee

knew that Byers had seen no drifters. That had been an excuse to lure him away from the Cowtown Hall dance.

And to pin Branch Craig's murder on him. . . .

This looked like it might be worth looking into. With Byers dead and buried, Dee had not a clue as to who had murdered Branch Craig.

Could Devil's Canyon provide some clues?

He sat Jones in high brush. He stood tall on stirrups to look about for possible enemies.

West, south and north stretched the lava rock plateau. Cold, forbidding, swept by eternal wind, brush bending with that wind.

Yonder trotted two coyotes, he noticed. They were about a quarter-mile apart. A dog and a bitch, out hunting. They killed mice and cottontails.

These two were the only living things he saw. He rode out of the brush and headed toward the uplift of Devil's Canyon a mile south.

He did not ride to he canyon's end. He hid Jones in high brush and went ahead on foot, carrying his rifle, bootheels making strong sounds on the flint.

He came to where the canyon lifted and became part of the plateau. Here were huge sandstone boulders. These hid him as he moved east along the canyon's north wall.

He worked his way to a point where old Wolf Nelson and Mark Stratton were directly below him in the gulch. Here his boots loosened a small boulder that tumbled downward, crashing through brush dotting the canyon-wall.

Dee hurriedly drew back into hiding. He took off his hat and looked around the corner of the sandstone rock behind which he crouched.

The boulder bounded down onto the gulch's sandy floor some fifty feet down-canyon from the wolfer and the saloon-keeper, then settled down.

Stratton looked up the canyon's wall, rifle in hand. He opened his mouth and said something that Dee did not hear because of the strong wind.

113

Dee pulled back his head. He waited patiently. Finally, he looked out again. Stratton stood over old Wolf, rifle at the ready. Old Wolf was digging in the sandy bottom of the canyon.

Dee was curious. What were they digging for? What did they talk about? Below was a ledge covered with brush. Carefully, keeping himself hidden behind boulders and brush, Dee Bowden worked his way downward, eyes glued on Stratton below—but Stratton did not look up.

Breathing heavily, sweating despite the cold wind, Dee reached the ledge without being seen. Hunkered, rifle across knees, he parted the brush and peered downward, noticing that now old Wolf dug in another spot.

Stratton and the old man were talking. Because of the wind and distance, Dee could not hear what they said. He could see their mouths moving, though.

He studied the terrain on all sides. He could move no closer to the pair. There was no protective brush—or boulders—between him and the two. He had to be content with where he was.

He craned his head, trying to pick up the words—but he couldn't.

Stratton jammed his rifle into his saddle's scabbard. He then stood over old Wolf Nelson with his .45 in hand.

One thing was plain: Stratton plainly was forcing the wolfer to dig. Dee Bowden scowled. Dig for what?

For money, maybe?

Branch Craig's stolen money? Money stolen from Craig after a cowardly bullet in his back had knocked him dead from saddle?

Dee's scowl deepened. Stratton wanted this money? Old Wolf knew where this money was buried?

This last assumption was the poser. Naturally, Stratton wanted money—more money. He was only human—or was he? But how-come old Wolf apparently knew where the money was buried?

Or did he know?

Old Wolf dug here, then there. He seemed confused. He raised his bottle, drank.

He looked wildly about. He looked like a trapped wild animal. Wind whipped his scraggly gray hair.

Plainly angry, Mark Stratton drew back a burly arm, fist hard and big. He was going to hit the old man. Old Wolf ducked.

Stratton held his blow, though. Stratton laughed.

Wolf pointed with his shovel to a service-berry bush. Stratton said something. Old Wolf moved to the bush's base. He began digging there.

Stratton began gathering twigs. He soon had a good fire burning on the sand. Old Wolf kept digging.

Suddenly, Stratton knocked the old man flat with one savage blow. Old Wolf's shovel went flying. Stratton leaped on the prone wolfer.

Stratton jerked loose two long rawhide thongs he carried under his gunbelt. Dee immediately recognized piggin' strings.

When a cowboy flanked a calf for the branding iron, he tied three of the calf's legs together with his thin, rawhide piggin' string. When wild calf-roping in a stampede, he also trussed three legs of the critter tightly together with his piggin' string which he carried in his teeth, rope whistling overhead.

Old Wolf kicked, bit, struck—but Stratton was too young, too heavy, too tough. And Stratton knew how to use piggin' strings.

He got the wolfer on his belly. He bent both of old Wolf's feet back, make a few fast circles, and the wolfer's legs were tied together at the ankles.

He rolled Wolf over. He put his knees on Wolf's shoulders. Within a few seconds, Wolf's hands were also tied in front of him at the wrists. Dee frowned. What the heck—"

Within seconds, all became clear.

Stratton dug out another piggin' string. He tied this

around the string on Wolf's wrist. With it, he pulled the man forward, Wolf sliding on his belly. He held Wolf's hands over the fire.

Stratton snarled something. Dee wished he was closer. He would have liked to know what Stratton had said.

Wolf shook his head.

Deliberately, Stratton pulled down on the piggin' string. Wolf's dirty hands went into the fire.

Wolf's mouth opened. He twisted, writhed, but Stratton held his wrists now, forcing the hands deeper into the fire.

Dee remembered hearing that Hank Byers' body had been burned. Now he figured he knew who had burned it. But still, he didn't know why. He could make a guess, but was his guess correct?

But he could stand no more of this. No human should treat another human in this terrible manner. His rifle rose to his shoulder. He took aim at Mark Stratton's black flat-brimmed hat lying ten feet beyond the saloon man on the sand.

Dee's .30-30 spat flame. Roar beat across the howling wind, echoing from canyon wall to canyon wall. The hat leaped, a sudden hole in its crown. And Mark Stratton leaped, too.

The saloon-man came hurriedly afoot. For one long second, he stared at the opposite canyon wall, thinking the shot had come from there. Dee realized the wind had played tricks.

The wind down there on the canyon's floor had made the report seemingly come from the opposite canyon wall. Already Mark Stratton's .45 pointed upward. The saloon-man shot at a boulder high on the southern slope of Devil's Canyon, and Dee was on the north slope.

Hurriedly, Stratton fell to one knee. This time, he would take more deliberate aim. He laid his six-shooter over his extended forearm but, before he could pull trigger, Dee Bowden again shot.

Grinning devilishly, Dee took aim at Stratton's

116

bootheel, stuck out behind the saloon-keeper, the boot's toe digging for purchase in the sand. It was a hard-to-do shot, an impossible shot. Dee allowed for the wind and distance, grin widening.

He squeezed the rifle's trigger.

The heel leaped from the boot.

Stratton leaped, too—straight upward. He pivoted, .45 pointing up at the hidden Dee. Lead whammed flint to ricochet madly into Wyoming space.

Dee counted five shots, then looked carefully around his boulder. An odd thing then happened. Dee had figured Stratton would leap into saddle minus hat and bootheel.

But, strangely, Stratton picked up both before leaping into saddle, whirling his horse and thundering down the canyon, reloading his pistol as he fled. Behind him, a startled old Wolf Nelson sat up, ankles and wrists still bound.

Old Wolf's mouth opened. He stared up at Dee's hiding place. His mouth opened again.

Plainly, the wolfer wanted this hidden sharp-shooter to come down and free him. This Dee Bowden was not going to do.

Dee looked down-canyon, Mark Stratton, bootheel and all, had reached the canyon's entrance. Even as Dee watched, Stratton disappeared from view, heading south under the rimrock's protective rim.

But he might circle, climb onto the plateau, and return—hoping to catch his assailant from behind, just as the assailant had caught him. Dee looked back at Old Wolf.

Old Wolf had freed his wrists. He sat untying his ankles and then got shakily to his feet.

He cupped his dirty hands to his whiskery mouth and hollered something, beady eyes raking the canyon's north wall. Dee kept hidden. Finally old Wolf dropped his hands.

Dee raised his .30-30 again. This time, he shot at old

Wolf's shovel. Steel howled under the impact of the bullet. His next shot landed two feet from old Wolf.

Old Wolf leaped, landing running. He picked up nothing, leaving his shovel behind. He landed on his mule and rode bent-over down canyon.

Dee sighted behind the laboring mule, but never pulled trigger. He couldn't afford to waste cartridges.

Old Wolf disappeared. Smiling broadly, Dee Bowden got to his feet, shoving fresh cartridges into his .30-30's magazine. He then climbed the canyon wall to where Jones awaited.

He swung into the Hamley.

Chapter Fourteen

Shorty Messenger sat a black gelding in the thick motte of chokecherry trees. "Why kill your cayuse with such speed, Dee?"

Dee reined in, Jones' hoofs sliding. "Yonder, Shorty? See that rider, headin' south along the rimrock?"

"Yeah. From here it looks like old Wolf Nelson on his mule, Sara."

"That's Wolf. From now on, you watch him. Never let him out of your sight for a moment."

Shorty studied his boss. "Do you feel well?"

Dee grinned. Quickly he told Shorty of Mark Stratton and Wolf Nelson in Devil's Canyon. "Wolf knows something Stratton wants to know. I think Branch Craig's money's buried in Devil's. Stratton sure as heck never had Wolf diggin' for water."

"I'll camp on Wolf's trail. There are some things you should know, boss." Shorty's eyes were on the far retreating Wolf Nelson. "I'll talk fast."

"Shoot, Shorty."

Last night Shorty had been in Round Rock's saloon, listening. "Stratton was in a poker game. Losin'. Mad. You're a man of many localities."

"Explain?"

"They claim now you kilt Byers. They claim you an' Byers made a deal to murder Branch, rob him. Then you wanted Byers' half. So you kilt him, Dee."

"Byers' body was burned?"

"You did that to get him to talk."

"Sheriff Watson— Issuin' another warrant a'gin me?"

"There's such talk."

Dee said, "You make me happy . . . like hell."

"You've been sighted all over. Jack Donner saw you yesterday seventy miles south on Willow Crick. Mike Swanson saw you eighty miles west on Risin' Butte. Jake Flores glimpsed you north sixty miles on Bitter Crick."

"I get aroun'," Dee said.

"The other day— When Watson kept me from seein' you, I met Jupp Gardiner. He was goin' into town to report somebody'd slugged him an' stole his lunch pail an' field-glasses."

"Slugged?"

Shorty gave details. Dee listened and hid his inner mirth. "Them field-glasses you pack, boss? Never seen 'em afore?"

"I've had 'em for years."

"What made the hole in the back of thet Hamley?"

"Hole? What hole?"

"I give up," Shorty said. "Oh, yes. Gardiner an' me rode out to look for that brock-faced four-year-old cow, that marker. The one Branch said you'd stole—an' the cow-buyer turned down—"

Dee could only frown.

"We rid all this range. Every coulee, draw. Thet cow is gone. Russled. Where you figger she was driven, Dee?"

"We've scouted miles aroun', Shorty. No ranch we know of has rustled stock on it. Rustled beef is goin' where there are mouths to eat it."

"An' where is them mouths, Dee?"

"Golden Gulch, mebbe?"

"Could be?"

Dee kept watching old Wolf, who now was a mere dot in distance. He told of seeing Banker Hendricks ride northwest.

'What'd you make of thet, Dee?"

"I'd say he was headin' for Golden Gulch."

"Why, boss?"

Dee shrugged. "I dunno. But I do know whatever it was that drug him out on the badlands in such cold weather was no good for somebody. Of course, I never have cottoned to the oily bastard."

"Count Stratton in on that, too," Shorty said. "Where next for you, Dee?"

"Golden Gulch."

Shorty said, "I'll be a burr in ol' Wolf's tail. Hey, Millie—"

"What about her, Shorty?"

"Leavin' town today. Gettin' the train out for Cheyenne. Said to say goodby to you."

For some reason, Dee Bowden felt a sense of loss. Millie's intervention had perhaps saved his life. "I liked her," Dee said.

Shorty said, "Ride a careful saddle, pal." He loped out of the brush and headed across the greasewood for the wagon-trail that would take him to old Wolf Nelson's miserable shack.

Then, Shorty did a queer thing. He dipped into a coulee and never came out opposite of where he rode in, and Dee soon saw the reason. A band of horsemen were riding the wagon-trail out of Round Rock.

Jupp Gardiner's field-glasses brought the posse into view. Sheriff Isaac Watson headed an even ten riders. Dee swung the glasses east. Within a short while Shorty rode out of the coulee far to the east.

Then, Shorty again cut across the greasewood for the wagon-trail, but this time the trail was to his west, not his south. To the posse he gave the appearance of riding in from Diamond inside a Diamond's eastern range.

The posse saw him, turned east, surrounded him. Dee saw Shorty pointing east. Soon the posse thundered through the sagebrush, headed east, and Shorty spurred on south.

Dee smiled.

Although Shorty had thrown Sheriff Watson's posse off-trail, Dee decided to take no chances by riding up Devil's Canyon to reach the high plateau, for Devil's Canyon might have riflemen staked out to shoot him from leather. Instead he would ride north thirty miles and thread his way up seldom-ridden Tanner's Canyon.

He made night camp ten miles north of Rafter V's home ranch. Darkness came early but just before full night set in he glimpsed a rider to the north. He reined in, dug out Gardiner's field-glasses, and put them on the horseman—which turned out to be a horse*woman*, not a horse*man*.

Despite the great distance, he recognized Nancy Craig's gaudy black and white pinto. The girl was heading north, also. Dee lowered his glasses, and frowned.

Night was nigh. Where was the girl going? Logically, had she ridden range that day she would have been *returning* to Rafter V and not riding away from it.

He thought of spurring Jones and trying to overhaul Nancy, but common sense told him she was too far away and night too close. The thought then came that perhaps she rode to visit some northern ranch.

Naturally, she'd ride to visit another woman or girl her age, Dee reasoned—but what northern ranch held such company? Rafter V's northern border was still miles and miles south.

The closest ranch north was some seventy odd miles away. And it had not a woman on it. Dee knew. Sim Rassmussen's childless wife had died a month ago, and there wasn't a woman on Bar S unless the old man had married again—a remote possibility.

He dared not light a fire. It might be seen by riders out hunting his head. He chewed cold jerky beef washed down by canteen-water. He knew that by morning Jones would be very thirsty. He poured the last water from the canteen into his battered old Stetson. The horse drank.

Wrapped in the sweaty saddle-blanket, back against a boulder, he slept fitfully, red dreams storming across his brain. Overhead, stars glistened—polished bits of fire suspended against black velvet.

Finally, dawn came. The cold sun inched over the eastern plain. Soon buckbrush and pines and spruce stood out in icy relief.

He was in saddle as the sun rose. The wind swept in from the northwest, harbinger of oncoming winter—and the wind was very cold. It cut through his heavy sheepskin to the marrow of his young bones.

Within him swelled a great and silent anger. He was a fugitive from the law. Unless he and his guns cleared the Bowden name, he would forever be wanted by the men of the badge, the bounty-hunters.

By now wanted-posters bearing his picture and description would be tacked up on saloon and post office walls in all of the Territory . . . and even beyond. He knew Sheriff Watson had had no trouble getting a photo of him for at the rodeo celebrating the railroad's coming many photos of cowboys had been taken by the railroad's photographer.

Naturally, the photographer had taken pictures of him, also.

Even if he fled this range—even if he abandoned all he'd worked his short life to accumulate—he would still be wanted. Were he to do this, he would never know a moment of peace. Each law officer he happened to meet might be the one who would attempt to arrest him, no matter in what territory or state he happened to inhabit.

He'd never leave this range. He'd clear up this trouble—this stigma against him and the Bowden name— or he'd die in the attempt.

He reached Tanner's Canyon at ten that morning. He knew the canyon well. A quarter-mile up-canyon was a spring that even in the longest dry spell had some water. Just beyond the springs Rafter V had strung a barbwire fence across the canyon to keep cattle from straying up the abyss to die from starvation on the grass-free mesa.

He dismounted at the springs. He removed Jones' bit.

The horse lowered his head and began to drink. Dee looked about.

What he saw made him suddenly draw to the down-canyon side of Jones. Thus if somebody up-canyon shot they'd have to shoot through his horse to hit him.

For the barbwire gate in the drift-fence had recently been opened, then closed. The loose earth told him that.

A man and horse had passed through the gate. Then the man had evidently tried to eradicate all tracks by sweeping the area with a wide leafy branch he'd evidently cut from some nearby tree.

He'd not done an efficient job. He'd left behind the fresh horse-droppings by sweeping them under a bush. Dee also saw a half of a horse imprint as the horse had started to climb the canyon's north wall.

He knew the rider had very recently passed through the gate. For one thing, the droppings were still fresh. For another, had the passing been some time before the canyon wind would have leveled all loose earth.

He judged the rider had opened the gate within the last thirty minutes. And he judged the rider was hidden on the north slope ahead.

A chill caught Dee Bowden's belly. Even now a rifle might be bearing down on him, hoping he'd move from behind Jones. He kept his head low, hiding it; only his legs showed beneath Jones' belly.

What should he do?

His first plan was to try to escape by galloping down-canyon. He soon discarded this. A rifle ball could send him rolling dead from leather, a bullet through his spine.

He realized he had but one way to go, and that way was up the canyon's south wall, using his horse as a shield.

But first he'd have to go through the gate.

Jones lifted his head. He'd drunk enough. It was time to move. Dee cocked his head, listening carefully. He heard only soughing of wind in a nearby box-elder. And usually the canyon was full of bird-song.

Using his horse as a shield, he somehow managed to

124

open the gate, lead Jones through, then close it again. Sweat clung to his forehead. He knew that at times during this procedure he'd been rather fully exposed, yet no bullet had whammed into his back.

He reasoned that the ambusher must then be located quite a distance up the canyon, for apparently the man did not trust a rifle shot from such distance to find its mark?

Plainly, the ambusher was waiting for a closer—and more certain—opportunity. And Dee was very sure an ambusher lurked ahead on the north slope.

His logic was simple. No trail ran up the canyon's north side. All was thick buckbrush, huge sandstones, and hard igneous rocks. No man except one seeking an ambush spot would even attempt to ride up the north wall.

A trail did run in on the south wall, though. It had been made by wildings coming down to the springs. Deer, elk, bear. Deer and elk nimbly leaped the barbwire; bears just climbed under.

Had this trail not been there, Dee would have fled down-canyon. His plan was to hang, one boot in stirrup, to the nigh side of Jones' saddle, the horse thus shielding most of his body while he ascended the south wall.

The trail was narrow. With Dee clinging to the bronc's left side, Jones began climbing, hoofs rasping flinty rock, muscles bunched as his powerful legs found purchase.

The horse seemed to climb very slowly. Dee clung to the front saddlestring, not exposing his hand by clinging to the saddle-horn. He had shot the heel from Mark Stratton's boot. The distance had been far. True, much luck had accompanied the bullet. The distance across the canyon was shorter than his shot had been.

He did not want to lose a hand.

Suddenly, Jones shied, almost leaving the narrow trail. Dee figured the horse had been shot, but he heard no report. He then saw a white-tail buck scrambling up-trail ahead. A deer had bounded from the brush.

Jones continued plodding. Dee continued clinging. He

did some mental deductions. Tanner's Canyon was a short canyon. He judged it about a mile long, no more.

A quarter-mile to the springs.... That left three-quarters of a mile of up-canyon. This steep trail did not run to the canyon's end. It reached the mesa area sooner.

Dee judged this trail to be between a half-mile and quarter-mile long. Jones plodded onward, Dee's weight on his left. Dee built more plans. Were his horse to be shot, he would reach over saddle, snake his Winchester .30-30 from boot and roll into the brush as Jones went down.

He knew he was putting a trusty mount in a precarious position. This bothered him. He glanced up-trail. He judged about fifty more yards to go. Once on the mesa—with the canyon's lip shielding him—he and Jones would be safe and—

And *maybe* there was no rifle pointing at his horse from the brush-choked north wall? Maybe—

Then, the bullet came.

It smashed into the saddle's fork. Jones started falling, then caught himself. The bullet had almost knocked the bronc down. What in the tarnation caliber did this ambusher shoot?

Dee heard a heavy, sodden roar. He realized the man had shot a .45-70 or a .45-90 rifle. Only a rifle of such caliber would pack such a great amount of lead, for the saddle's fork was shattered badly.

Jones found footing. He snorted, leaped ahead, stumbled, fell—and Dee rolled into the buckbrush, Winchester .30-30 in hand.

A bullet whammed off a boulder behind him. He landed on his belly, rifle over a big rock as he pointed it north. A wisp of black smoke hung across the canyon, curling upward from a clump of buffalo-berry bushes.

Above him, Jones scrambled afoot, reins trailing. The horse trotted up the trail, head to one side so he'd not step on his reins. He did not limp. Dee's heart lifted. His mount was solid and whole.

Jones disappeared over the canyon's rim. Dee knew the bronc would stop there and try to graze what little foliage there was, despite his bit. Dee turned his attention to the ambusher.

He figured that this bushwhacker had seen him riding toward Tanner's Canyon. The ambusher had then ridden ahead to hole up to kill him. Dee had kept a careful watch of the trail ahead, too. But the man could have sneaked up a draw or coulee to enter the canyon unnoticed.

He did not shoot at the area below the rifle-smoke. To do so would undoubtedly be a mere waste of .30-30 cartridges. Although Shorty had given him .45 and .30-30 bullets he still did not have too many. And he might get into a real shootout on the trail ahead.

And it was better to start saving from the top instead of the bottom, he knew.

Who on this range shot a .45-90 or .45-70? He knew of only one man—Jim North.

Again the big rifle threw a hunk of lead across Tanner's Canyon. Once again black powdersmoke hung over bushes.

This time, though, the ambusher had fired behind bushes further up-canyon. Although he had peered hard, Dee had not seen his assailant move. Brush had hidden the rifleman.

Dee did not return the fire. He wormed his way upward, landing behind another big boulder. He hoped to work to the canyon's rim, unseen, for from that high point he could look down on his hunter.

Another big chuck of lead whammed noisily across the canyon, ricocheting harmlessly. Dee grinned ironically. Were this hidden man really Jim North then North had really shot a gaping hole in his new Hamley saddle!

Dee worked upward, keeping hidden; at last, he reached the canyon's top. Here was a space of fifteen feet without brush or boulders. Rifle in hand, heart in throat, he scrambled upward knowing he was in full view of the hidden rifleman.

The huge rifle boomed. Sand and gravel spurted upward three feet below Dee's digging boots. Dee slipped, threatened to slide back. He caught his footing, and with a great heave, went over the canyon's rim, a bullet singing over him.

He landed sprawled out on the level ground, the canyon's lip shielding him from further view. His breath tore from his lungs and he lay for a moment on his belly, recovering his wind and logic.

Crouched, he ran west ten yards, noting that Jones stood hiphumped in safety to his left. Then he dropped to his belly, wormed to the canyon's edge—and looked down into the abyss.

First, he saw the rifleman's horse. He recognized it immediately. The wind-broken bay of Jim North's he'd stolen from the Round Rock livery-barn stood deep in a grove of young saplings.

The horse was hidden from anybody in the canyon. Dee saw it only because he was high above it.

His gaze moved slowly up and down the canyon's brush-covered walls. Where was the horse's rider? He carefully studied the area from whence had come the last rifle shots.

He saw nobody in that section. He continued looking. Finally, he made out the rifleman.

The man crouched behind a boulder, rifle lying over the top of the big rock. Dee could see only his head and shoulders. He needed his field glasses. Cautiously, he pulled back and, when the rim of the canyon hid him from eyes below, he straightened and ran to Jones.

The glasses showed Jim North clearly.

Grinning, Dee put down the glasses. He laid his Winchester over a ledge and took careful aim at a huge rock at the bronc's right. Then he squeezed the trigger. The rifle kicked back against his shoulder.

A hard-nosed .30-30 bullet richocheted off the flinty rock with a mad, howling sound. Instantly, the horse

128

came alive. The first bullet made the bay rear in surprise, forelegs fighting air.

The horse's reins were tied to the branch of a bullberry tree. His rearing broke the branch. Dee shot closer the second time. The bronc whirled and tore up-slope, dragging the limb behind him.

Hurriedly, Dee drew back. Overhead whistled a huge hunk of lead. Crouched, hidden, Dee ran east some fifty yards, then crept again to the canyon's ledge—and now he was directly opposite Jim North.

North stood up, his horse thundering past on the flat ground above, the bullberry branch still tied to his reins. Dee took careful aim. He did not want to kill the ambusher, although had he had the chance North would surely have killed him.

He shot at the boulder in front of North. The bullet yammered into space, singing a high-pitched lethal song. Dee's second bullet hammered loose rock directly behind the boots of the hard-scrambling North, for North was desperately climbing the slope to escape.

Rifle in hand, he made a comical figure, boots sliding in shale as his feet slipped in his mad desire for more speed. From Dee's vantage, North looked like a huge crab, arms spread out, feet digging—and Dee grinned as he shot again, this time throwing dust on North's rump.

North screamed, "Don't kill me! I got a wife an'—"

His words came clearly across the canyon's clean air and died as he finally reached the ridge, and safety. A few moments later Dee saw him thunder east on his bay, whipping the bronc for more speed.

Dee sat down reloading. His weapon replenished with cartridges, he stood up just in time to see North and the windbroken bay drop over the rimrock, heading for the safety of Round Rock Basin.

Grinning, Dee went to Jones. North's bullet had made quite a hole in the Hamley's fork. Dee swung up, grabbed the saddle-horn, pulled back. All was firm. The saddle-tree's bars had not been broken.

He jammed his rifle, barrel down, into the saddle scabbard, wishing now he'd not given over to impulse and wasted so many shots at the bay and its owner. Then, he remembered seeing North madly scrambling upward, and he decided the bullets had been well spent.

He turned Jones northwest toward Golden Gulch.

Chapter Fifteen

At full gallop, the blue roan stud stumbled over an exposed sagebrush root. He fell full length, throwing his rider. When he scrambled afoot he held his nigh foreleg off the ground.

Getting to his feet, Banker John Hendricks brushed dust and twigs from his neat gray suit, realizing he'd broken no bones. He cursed the horse's clumsiness and drew back a boot, preparatory to kicking the beast in the belly—and then he noticed the nigh foreleg.

He didn't kick.

Anger changed to curiosity. Was the leg broken? Would he have to shoot the stud? Curiosity changed to fear.

Scowling, he looked about.

He and the horse were two small ants located on a flat area so large its limits ran beyond the range of his eyes. All he saw was sagebrush, greasewood and alkali deserts that stretched all directions until his eyes met only the far dim gray-blue of absolute vision.

His glance at the sun judged the hour to be around three. A man on foot in this inhospitable wilderness— He walked to the roan. He said, "How's the leg, Roany?"

The roan, of course, had no reply.

Hendricks led the horse. The horse limped badly. At first, he could hardly touch the dried soil with his hoof. As he walked, he limbered up slightly; still, he had a bad limp.

Hendricks wiped sweat from his forehead, shoving back his expensive beaver Stetson. He should have taken another horse with him. Led one and rode one and changed mounts every two or three hours, like Mark Stratton had advised him.

He silently cursed his stupidity. They claimed a man learned from experience. He doubted this. He made the same error over and over again and knew it was an error when making it.

When he and Stratton had broken out of the pen. . . . They'd led one bronc, ridden the other, changed mounts. . . .

He shoved that remembrance aside.

He walked a mile, leading his roan. Gradually, the horse used his bum leg more; evidently he'd pulled a shoulder-muscle. Finally, Hendricks figured the roan could carry his weight.

He lifted himself gently into the saddle, thankful he was not a heavy man. He rode slowly northwest, always northwest.

The roan gradually became more foot-sure. Within two miles, he could seek a trot; another mile, he could gallop. Hendricks let the horse lope only a short distance, though.

He pulled the roan down to a running-walk that caused the miles to fall behind. The sun sank lower. The sun set with the wind growing even colder. Ahead were some huge sandstones.

He decided to camp in their windbreak. He stripped the roan and picketed him out with his lariat for the rocks had held a bit of summer rain from running off and therefore had a little grass at their bases.

He carried a Sioux waterbag—a long steer-gut filled with water—tied over the back saddle-skirts. He allowed some of this water to trickle into his Stetson.

The horse drank noisily, nostrils flaring. Hendricks washed his face lightly with the remaining water, then drank himself. He then undid a buckskin bag's thongs.

The bag contained cuts of pemmican.

These would be his supper. He had bought the pemmican from a Shoshoni squaw in Round Rock. One bite told him the squaw had used chokecherry instead of bullberry in making the pemmican.

He preferred bullberries. Bullberries gave the pemmican a more substantial flavor. Sunset rapidly became night. He wrapped himself in the heavy woolen Hudson's Bay blanket.

He spent a cold, miserable night. His blanket had not been enough. During the night, the wind increased in intensity and coldness. His feet were cold in his Justin boots.

The roan, too, was stiff. He limped more than he had when finishing his run last night. Gradually, the bronc limbered up. Soon deep snow would cover this section of Wyoming. The snow would make all rustling stop. Cattle could be trailed by hoofprints in snow.

He realized he was behind schedule. That bad fall had set his timetable back. Usually he covered the eighty miles between Round Rock and Golden Gulch in two and one-half days.

Now it would take three. He pulled his head lower in the high sheepskin collar of his sheepskin coat. He had his neckscarf tied around his head to protect his ears.

He said to the roan, "I've had enough of this goddamned cold worthless country. You an I part company soon, Roany."

The roan loped on, dodging around high sagebrush. He remembered talking seriously to Mark Stratton the other day.

"One hundred thousand in my bank, Mark. Sucker money that the sucker's will never get back."

"My saloon's paid for itself and then some, too. What's on your mind, fellow convict?"

"Go easy on that convict crap! What if somebody heard you?"

"Nobody but us two aroun'." Stratton's face showed

momentary anger. "What's on your mind, John?

"Southern California."

Stratton smiled. "I'm with you. There the weather fits a man's clothes, they tell me. A Texas blizzard is bad but it's soon over. Here there's nine months of blizzard and three months of scorchin' hot sun."

"There'll be snow soon."

They talked in Hendricks's quarters behind his bank. The banker walked to the window. He looked out on a dusty alley littered with trash. He spoke over a bony shoulder.

"No more Byers.... Hank's down there lookin' up at the sagebrush roots, not a horseback looking down."

"More money for you an' me."

"One more raid, after this."

Stratton got to his feet. He was big, hard, tough. "Suits me, John. Cy reported in. Him an' his three are hittin' Diamon' inside a Diamon' now with Bowden runnin'."

Hendricks turned. His brows lifted. "I haven't seen Cy since the last pay-off in Golden Gulch. That was three weeks ago to the day. What day did he report in?"

Stratton scowled, then said, "Monday, in my saloon. Said he'd tried your door first but nobody home."

"Monday...."

"Monday night," Stratton said.

Hendricks smiled. "My night to court the Widow Smith. What'd Cy say?"

"Herd was bein' built up. Rafter V an' Diamon' inside a Diamon' stock, the first time we've hit Bowden's cattle. Asked me to tell you to be in Golden Gulch by next Friday."

Hendricks asked, "How do things look to you?"

"Same as ever. Safe. This sher'ff... Brains is where his saddle's seat fits his skinny carcass. Only fly in the ointment is that wolfer, Nelson. An' he'll tell where that money is or I'll pull his big gut out an inch at a time to toast it."

"Get that money, Mark."

134

"I'll get it."

Suddenly, Hendricks now reined in the roan, standing on stirrups to stare at a moving object far ahead—a small dark object plainly coming his direction. Was it a horse? Or a cow?

He discreetly reined his roan onto a slight rise where, hidden by high sagebrush, he trained his field-glasses on the object. The powerful lens brought the object closer.

Hendricks then saw that this was a lone cow headed southeast, coming directly toward him. His frown deepened. He had made this trip a number of times and never before had he seen a domestic animal on it except his own saddle-horse.

What was a cow doing on this grass-free wilderness?

He rode out to intercept the beast. Even the cowthieves did not move cattle over this wilderness. They swung north along the rimrock and then took Hell Gate Canyon northwest to come out on Shotgun Mesa, the north rim of this desolation.

The cow walked rapidly. Upon seeing the horseman, the beast began loping, heading southeast. Hendricks spurred his roan closer. The cow bore the Diamond inside a Diamond brand.

Hendricks reined-in his horse. The cow loped on, then fell to a long walk. She seemed to know where she was going. And she seemed determined to get there, Hendricks thought.

Hendricks rubbed his jaw thoughtfully. Dee Bowden's cow.... Brock-faced cow who had evidently been separated from her calf.... and was plainly hurrying back to her home-range for that calf.

John Hendricks suddenly understood. Cy Zachary and his three rustlers had driven this Bowden cow off Round Rock range with other stolen Bowden cattle.

Somehow, this cow had escaped. Now she loped across country to her home range and her calf.

Hendricks quickly pulled his .25-35 from saddle boot. Standing on stirrups, he sent the rifle to his shoulder,

135

sights finding the distant cow. He fired three times.

The cow did not falter. She dipped out of sight in a brush-filled coulee a half-mile away.

Hendricks knew he had missed. The distance had been too far for the small rifle. He wished he'd taken a .30-30 from the rack, and left the .25-35 home. But he liked the smaller rifle.

Lighter, easier to handle....

One thing was sure: that brockle-faced roan cow should never be allowed to reach Bowden range. She'd come down Devil's Canyon and be stopped at Bowden's drift fence.

Bowden or that bastardly cowboy of his—that Shorty Messenger— would see the cow on the opposite side of the drift fence, bawling to get through. And each would then think: How'd that cow get on that side of the drift-fence?

And the cow was a Bowden marker. His mind went back to Branch Craig and Bowden going for guns that hectic day in Stratton's Diamond Willow. Craig had claimed a cow—one of his markers—now wore a worked-over Rafter V brand.

The cow had to be killed!

Hendricks settled in leather and hit his roan with his savage star-roweled spurs, intending to run the cow down and kill her, but the horse stumbled again over a greasewood root.

This time, the roan did not fall full length; he merely went to his knees. Hendricks held to his saddle and was not thrown and the horse scrambled to all fours.

But he did not move. He just stood with his nigh front-leg held off the ground.

Angrily, Hendricks spurred the beast. The horse tried to move and then almost fell again. He stopped. The rowels failed to move him. Hendricks quit spurring.

The banker dismounted. He cursed the roan. The roan stood still, leg still raised.

Hendricks tried to lead the animal. It limped terribly.

136

Man and horse moved on, the man on foot. The impotent endless sky looked mercilessly down. The horse failed to walk better. Hendricks knew then the cow would escape. He cursed his bad luck.

He took his thoughts off the brockle-faced cow. He put them on the miles ahead. He added this to that and decided that Cyrus Zachary and his three cow-thieves might be in Hell Gate Canyon.

How many miles to Hell Gate? He judged about fifteen. Upon stealing Round Rock cattle, the stock was driven directly north along the base of the rimrock for some forty odd miles.

Then the rustled beef was pointed up Hard Rock Canyon which lifted onto this god-forsaken endless mesa to finally dip down into Hell Gate Canyon, then on to Golden Gulch and the slaughter house.

Usually Cy Zachary held the stolen beeves in Hell Gate a day or so to rest them so they'd have more fat on them when they went under the butcher's knife. Cy and his three men *might be* in Hell Gate....

The roan's condition puzzled Hendricks. He carefully felt along the leg. Apparently no bones were broken, but yet the leg did not improve. Were it not for the fact that he would have to carry his saddle he would have shot the animal. As it was, the roan could not carry Hendricks.

Man and animal moved slowly across the wilderness. That night Hendricks again spent a cold, miserable night. Next morning the roan was no better. Noon found the man on the ledge overlooking Hell Gate Canyon.

His bloodshot eyes searched the canyon below. Usually Cy Zachary held the stolen herd directly below for here the canyon spread out and made a grazing area.

But no cattle grazed below. No rustlers with ready rifles guarded each lip of the canyon. Nor was one stationed below to kill anybody trailing the beef.

Hendricks then realized this meadow below was not the one used by Cy Zachary as a way-station. Where was the herd? Had it already passed through Hell Gate?

Where was the meadow usually used by the rustlers? The canyon ran east and west.

Was the meadow to the west? Or was it eastward? Hendricks realized he was bone-weary and slightly confused. He looked about for land marks. He saw nothing but endless wastelands.

No buttes or mountains or hills marred the horizon in any direction. There came to him that there was but one thing to do. He would drop down into Hell Gate.

The canyon's bottom would tell him if cattle had recently passed over it going west. He found a dim trail winding downward. Evidently deer and wildings had made the trail. He judged there would be a water-hole—or a spring—at the trail's end in the canyon's floor.

The roan descended with difficulty but finally man and beast were on the canyon's floor. The sandy bottom showed many head of cattle had recently gone west.

Hendricks knew the cattle had pased within a few hours for the harsh canyon wind was already leveling all tracks. Hendricks and horse started west.

Hendricks came upon some cattle-droppings. He gingerly poked one yellow pancake with a stick. It had crusted over but the interior was mushy.

He threw the twig away. He judged the cattle to have passed through this area yesterday evening. He continued west, leading the limping roan. He walked for about four hours.

He was very tired. He was not used to much walking. Would he ever find Cyrus Zachary and the herd? Had Cy driven on and not stopped to rest? Was he heading with the herd directly to Golden Gulch?

Then, he heard a cow bawl. His heart lifted. He rounded a bend and then a man rode out of the brush, rifle across saddle. Beyond the rider grazed stolen Diamond inside a Diamond and Rafter V cattle, scattered up and down Hell Gate Canyon.

The rider was about Hendricks' age. He was bearded, blocky, tough-looking. He packed a six-shooter on each

138

hip. He loafed in saddle, boots dangling free of stirrups.

"Saw you comin', John. Expected you yesterday. What's the trouble with the roan?"

Hendricks explained.

Cyrus Zachary nodded. "Ol' convict pal, there's only one thing to do with that cayuse."

The banker hesitated. The roan had carried him many miles since he had come to Round Rock. "He's a good horse."

"He was a *good* horse," Cyrus Zachary corrected.

Hendricks shrugged. "As you say."

They left the roan behind and walked up-canyon, Zachary leading his bronc. They came out of the high buckbrush and ahead was the stolen herd, grazing on the short grass.

A rustler rode up. He was in his twenties, bearded, gun tied down on his narrow hip.

Zachary said, "John's roan. Back yonder. Shoulder out, I'd say. You got a rifle. Use it."

"Okay, boss."

The cowboy's bay gelding started down-canyon. Cyrus Zachary caught him by the reins, stopping him. "The girl?"

"Still hogtied. Layin' yonder ag'in the canyon wall, where you left her." The cowboy rode east.

The banker looked at his former cell-mate. "What girl?"

Zachary didn't answer. He only grinned. He and the banker walked to the canyon's north wall. Here, lying out of the wind, was a young woman, hands tied behind her, ankles trussed.

She glared up at Hendricks. "So you're in on this rustling, too, banker?" Sarcasm dripped from her voice.

Hendricks hid his surprise. He looked down at her, mind busy. This *had* to be the last raid. Somehow, he'd have to get word to Stratton down in Round Rock. Stratton would have to make tracks out, fast.

"Where'd you get her?"

"Trailed us up Hell Gate. Had to run her down an' tie her an' take her along."

Hendricks could only nod. This captured woman changed the setup completely. He heard a rifle shot from down-canyon.

Only one shot, no more.

The roan was finished.

"What're you going to do with her?" the banker asked.

"Slim made an error when he merely captured her. He should have shot her from saddle."

Again, the banker nodded.

"So we decided to hold her until you came and to see what you thought of, John."

Hendricks summoned a small smile, eyes still on the trussed-up woman. Finally he said, "How are you, Miss Craig?"

Nancy spat at him.

Chapter Sixteen

Two hours out of Tanner's Canyon, Dee Bowden came across the brock-faced cow heading for the beginning of Devil's Canyon.

The critter was tired and mean. She tossed her long horns angrily. Slobber hung from her jaws. She breathed deeply, ribs rising and falling. She plainly had traveled far and fast.

Dee pulled in Jones. He sat saddle, watching the cow pass. He made no effort to stop her. He noticed she had blood on her left hip. To him it looked as if a rifle or shortgun bullet had broken her tough hide there.

Dee Bowden scowled. How had the cow got on this west side of the canyons' drift fences? Had somebody shot at her?

He came to only one conclusion: the cow had been driven off Round Rock range. She had not wandered off onto this high, grassless plateau. She had been choused out of the basin by rustlers.

And she somehow had manged to bunch-quit and make it home again. He looked northwest over the terrain the cow plainly had just covered. If his logic were correct, somewhere far ahead should be a rustled herd—and that herd evidently contained some of his Diamond inside a Diamond cattle?

He did not swing in behind the cow to trail her to the Devil's Canyon. She could drink from the springs by inserting her head between the barbwires. Dee Bowden rode northwest, trailing the cow's hoof-prints.

Mack Weston had orders to ride each canyon and check on the drift fences each day. He'd open the gate and let the cow back onto Round Rock grass. With Shorty Messenger watching old Wolf Nelson, Weston would be the only man holding down Diamond inside a Diamond's home-ranch buildings.

Dee pulled his head down lower in his sheepskin's high collar, eyes on the brockle-faced cow's tracks, thinking of Shorty, who at that moment should be guarding old Wolf.

Shorty was, indeed, guarding the old wolfer. He was, in fact, sitting in Wolf's old shack, back to the hot pot-bellied heater, talking to the wolfer, who lay on his stinking bunk between two of his lanky, muscular coyote hounds. "You're sure not usin' the brains God gave you," Shorty said.

"Maybe He never guv me none?"

Shorty disregarded that. "You know where Branch Craig's money is buried. An' unless I'm terribly wrong, you know who shot an' kilt Branch Craig."

"How come you know all this?"

Shorty told the old man that it was Dee Bowden's rifle that shot the heel off Mark Stratton's boot to send the saloon-keeper running out of Devil's Canyon.

"If'n Dee hadn't shot, you'd have burned like Byers," Shorty said.

"So Bowden was who saved me, huh? Why?"

"He likes you, I guess."

"He shot my shovel. Put a hole through that spring steel, his rifle did. My shovel's still in Devil's."

"Why don't you take me to where Craig's money is in the Canyon?"

Old Wolf laughed. "How are you, Bingo?" He spoke to the cur on his left. Bingo's tail beat the dirty bedding. Wolf plainly ignored Shorty's question.

Shorty said, "You ol' bastard."

142

Old Wolf bristled immediately. "I'm no bastard, buster. My ma an' pa was legally married. You beat the hell outa North for him callin' you a bastard! I might tangle fisticuffs with you!"

"I'm more than ready, ol' man."

Wolf settled back. "Why you stickin' aroun' my cabin? I never done invited you."

"To keep Stratton from killin' you," Shorty said.

"Why would Stratton want to kill me? If he kilt me I couldn't tell him—" The ancient clipped his jaw shut.

Shorty laughed. "Then you admit you know where Craig's money is buried?"

"I admit nothin', cowboy."

Shorty enjoyed the heat on his back. "I'm goin' sleep in your shack, too—that is, if I kin stan' the stink."

"I never invited you. I don't want you aroun'."

"You'll have to put up with me, or you'll be burned as bad as Byers was—or dead?"

"Dead?"

"Sure thing, ol' man. You tell where thet money is hid an' then Stratton'll kill you. He has to. He has to keep you silent."

Wolf Nelson scowled, rubbing the ears of Jingle, his right-hand hound. "You got a point," he finally admitted.

"You oughta tell all to Sher'ff Watson."

"Watson? Watson's a fool!"

Shorty shrugged. "Who isn't?"

"You're crazy. I'm goin' to sleep."

"Your dogs already are asleep."

Soon the wolfer began to snore. One dog was awakened by the raucous snorning. He got off the bed and crawled under it. Shorty dozed in his rawhide-backed home-made chair, the heat from the round stove feeling good. Without knowing it, he too slipped off to sleep.

He was awakened by the sound of hoofs stopping before the door. Atuomatically he reached for his pistol-grip but withdrew his hand when a masculine voice called, "Shorty?"

"Inside, Mack."

Ruddy-faced Mack Weston entered, slipping off his mittens. He nodded toward snoring Wolf Nelson. "Drunk ag'in, huh?"

"Man's downfall, Mack. Along with women, of course."

"I'd like to fall a few notches lower. Where's his bottle?"

Shorty shook his head. "Dee ordered absolutely no booze, remember?"

"But Dee ain't here an'—"

"Dee's still the boss, no matter where he is."

"Okay," Mack said, "Okay. Hey, that brock-faced cow returned."

"She did. Where'd you see her?"

Mack told about finding the cow on the up-canyon side of the Devil's Canyon drift-fence.

"How'd she get up-side?" Shorty wanted to know.

"I don't know. She's got a kinda cut along her off hip, too. I roped her an' throwed her an' doused it with tar."

"Cougar mebbe jumped her?"

"Naw, looks more like a bullet groove. I think somebody's shot at her an' jes' nicked her."

"Who t'heck would wanna shoot thet cow?"

Mack Weston lifted heavy shoulders under his sheepskin overcoat. "Dunno, Shorty. But this range has gone nuts." He looked out the door. "What's the saloon-keeper doin' out in this col' wind?"

"You got me," Shorty said.

Mark Stratton's expensive saddle was cinched on his favorite mount—a blazed-faced sorrel gelding. The well-oated bronc pulled at the cruel spade bit, fighting it every inch of the way.

Stratton came down, star-rowels jingling. He was big, hard, tough in a blue sheepskin overcoat. A downward glance told Shorty that Stratton had visited the town bootmaker. Both boots sported new heels.

Stratton said, "The ol' man— He sick?"

Shorty nodded. "Howcome you ride away from a hot stove on a day this cold?"

"You're inquisitive," Stratton snapped. "Have either of you seen the Craig girl?"

"Should we have?" Shorty asked.

Stratton's wind-red face grew tougher. "No smart answers, cowpoke, please. A cow-buyer rode down from Blasted Stone to the Rafter V to buy some stock. Nancy wasn't home."

"Okay," Shorty said, "she wasn't home. What're you leadin' up to?"

"They said at Rafter V that she'd ridden into town to check school records, seein' schools goin' start so soon, but she never reached town. One Rafter V hand said he'd seen her from a distance yesterday afternoon late. An' she was ridin' north."

Shorty and Mack exchanged glances. There was something here neither could understand. "Why you so interested in Nancy Craig?"

"Hell, there's a killer loose on this range. Her father was shot down—shot in the back—from ambush. We all know who shot an' killed him. An' I figger the daughter isn't safe with Dee Bowden around, either."

Shorty held his temper. Mack Weston doubled his fists but remained silent.

"You got any idea where Bowden is?" Stratton asked.

"I don't know where he is but he's out huntin' down cattle-rustlers," Shorty said. "One rustled cow come home this mornin'."

"Rustled cow— Came home?"

Shorty told the saloon-keeper about the brockle-faced cow. "What does that signify?" Stratton asked.

"She's been driv off'n Diamon' inside a Diamon' range. She's escaped the russlers an' come hellbent for home, maybe?"

Shorty watched Stratton's wide face. The saloon-keeper had summoned his poker-face which showed no emotion.

"Lot's of maybes," Stratton said.

"Could be," Shorty said. "Heard you an ol' Wolf here had a session in Devil's Canyon, with him workin' around' with a shovel?"

"Who told you that?"

"A little bird."

"Your little bird—" Stratton caught himself. "What the hell you drivin' at, cowpoke?"

"Got two new heels, an' you needed only one."

Stratton said, "Dee Bowden?"

Shorty nodded. "Good rifle shot, huh? How come you get two new heels when you only needed one? An' you took the heel Dee shot along with you? Was it beyon' repair?"

"Just what are you doin' here, cowboy?"

Shorty had his hand on his holstered .45's grip. "I'll tell you, Stratton. Dee stationed me here to pertect ol' Wolf."

Stratton's face was still poker-deadpan. "Pertect him from who?"

"From you. He saw you try to make toast out of the ol' man's hands. He remembered Byers bein' bad burned."

Stratton said, "I'd pull against you but it'd be like stealin' candy from a kid, Messenger. I came out here to bargain with ol' Wolf about buying a batch of his whiskey but that can wait—"

He strode to his sorrel, hooked his nigh-stirrup, shot his ornate boot into it and swung up. Without a word, he swung the sorrel and loped back toward Round Rock, tough in leather.

He dipped into a coulee, fell from view. Shorty looked at Mack Weston. They were silent for a long moment and then Weston said, "He's riled, Shorty. What's next?"

Shorty rubbed his jaw. "Danged if I know rightly, Mack. Odd thing, the banker ain't in town. Ol' Snowden said that when he rode out for booze this mornin'."

"Jupp Gardiner an' me met as I rid down here. Jupp said in town they said the banker rode south."

Shorty looked at old Wolf, who still lay on his back but

146

did not now snore. "This ol' bastard knows more than he wants to tell."

Wolf's eyes opened. "Thanks for the compleement, Shorty. Yeah, I lissened to the whole discussion. It proved interestin'."

"When you goin' tell me where thet money is buried?" Shorty asked.

Wolf swung skinny legs around and sat on the bed's edge. He reached under the bed. A dog there snarled. The wolfer cursed him. His hand groped. Finally he came out with a jug of whiskey, full to the cork.

Tobacco-discolored teeth removed the cork. The jug lifted, cracked lips curled—fiery home-distilled alcohol tumbled and frolicked down the leathery throat, the Adam's Apple dancing in joy.

Mack Weston and Shorty Messenger stared in wonder. The jug hung in space and seemingly never would come down.

"A slug that big of thet stuff'd kill me," Mack Weston said.

Shorty said, "He's got a goat's belly. He can even eat a tin-can."

Finally, the jug came down. Old Wolf wiped his mouth with the back of a filthy hand. "Jes' a little snort," he said and then, to Shorty, "You stick with me, Messenger, an' I'll learn you how to make good firewater."

"I'm willin'," Shorty said.

Mack Weston pulled on his mittens. "I gotta get back to the ranch. Still got the danged milk cows to strip. What'd you think about this Nancy disappearin', Shorty?"

"If she's dead, Dee never kilt her."

"I know that. He never kilt Craig, either." Mack Weston looked sharply at Wolf Nelson. "Who kilt Branch Craig, Wolf?"

"Aimed to catch me off'n my guard, huh?" Wolf Nelson cackled. "Well, gotta look at my mash. Wanna come, Shorty?"

"Okay."

Mack Weston looked at the whiskey jug. He wet his lips.

"Ride into town tomorrow mornin' an' keep your eyes open and ears not covered an' then report back to me," Shorty told Mack Weston. "An' quit eyein' thet jug like a hungry dog eyein' a gut wagon. None of it's fer you."

Mack Weston mounted and spurred north toward Diamond inside a Diamond. Old Wolf and Shorty followed a well-worn path through the willows of Doggone Creek to Old Wolf's still.

Weston reported in at eight the next morning. The entire Round Rock country was up in arms over Nancy Craig's disappearance. Most of its residents were sure Dee Bowden had killed the heiress and buried her.

"I tol' some Dee'd have no reason to kill Nancy," Weston said, "an' they got real mad at me. I thought for a while they'd gang-up on me!"

"Kill fever," Wolf Nelson said.

Shorty spoke to the wolfer. "Dee figures you know who kilt Craig, like I said. You know Dee purty well, I take it?"

Wolf took a long swig and, when his bottle was lowered, said, "Danged right I know Dee. Knowed him since he was a button on Mrs. Rothwell's knee. Think a heap of him, too."

"They catch him an' they'll string him up," Mack Weston said gloomily.

Old Wolf blinked. He'd slept between four hounds that night. He stunk of dog, whiskey and filth. "Right never thought of that," he said slowly. "They'd be hangin' a man who's—"

He stopped speaking.

After a while Shorty said, "You never finished your sentence, Wolf. Continue, please?"

Wolf cackled loudly. "Ain't got a thing more to say."

Mack gestured Shorty outside. Old Wolf stayed in the shack. Mack said, "That tinhorn saloon-keeper's gone.

148

Rode out last night. Pancho Martinez is runnin' the joint."

"But Pancho's the saloon swamper," Shorty said.

"He's runnin' it now. Said Stratton tol' him to. Pancho says Stratton didn't say where he was goin' or how long he'd be gone."

Shorty scowled. "Go on."

Mack swung into saddle. He leaned low. "Pancho tol' me on the quiet that lots of Stratton's clothes are gone from his quarters upstairs. Pancho forced the door and went in."

"How many hosses did Stratton take?"

"I talked to ol' Jake at the Town Livery Barn. Jake said Stratton's blazed-faced sorrel is gone and so is a hoss belongin' to the banker. Jake figures Stratton took that hoss along."

"Pack horse," Shorty murmured. "I think Stratton's gone for good. Has thet banker come back?"

"Not yet. Thet ol' cashier of Hendricks'—what's his name—is runnin' the bank, they tell me. What'd you read into it?"

"One thing for sure, Mack. I'm not goin' tell ol' Wolf thet Stratton's gone. I got t'hol' the threat of Stratton over him."

"I figgered that, Shorty. Thet's why I got you outside to talk to you. This thing is drawin' to a head, huh?"

"Let's hope so," Shorty said.

Mack Weston again rode toward Diamond inside a Diamond. Shorty tried to get the wolfer to eat something but old Wolf said he always drank his breakfast. Shorty sat and talked to the old man. At eleven Sheriff Watson and three possemen rode up.

"Call the sher'ff in," Wolf Nelson told Shorty.

Sheriff Watson entered. "Lord, it stinks in here!" He looked at Shorty Messenger. "You move in with Wolf?"

"Wolf's my bes' friend," Shorty said. "You a-huntin' Dee, sher'ff?"

"Yeah, an' Nancy, too. Yeah, an' whoever robbed

Hendricks' bank last night of every red cent it had. An' murdered the ol' Sig Livingston, too."

Shorty could only stare. Old Wolf looked up, mouth agape.

"Bank didn't open at usual time this mornin'," the lawman said. "So we investigated. Had to force the door open. Odd thing, too—whoever sneaked in must've had a key, 'cause no door was forced until we forced one."

"Maybe whoever did it called the ol' man to the door?" Shorty said. "Then when the door was open—"

"Could be."

"Banker Hendricks— Where's he?" old Wolf asked.

"Left town a day or so ago, they tell me. Rid south but for where I don't know. Everybody says Dee Bowden kilt the ol' man, robbed the money."

"Why'd they say that?" Shorty asked.

"They claim Dee might have decided to leave the country. An' he needed money—"

"Hogwash!" Shorty said.

"Any clues as to what happened to Nancy?" Wolf Nelson asked.

"Yesterday afternoon I put three Shoshoni bucks on her trail. They looked at the tracks left by her paint in the Rafter V corral. One even got down and smelled the tracks."

Shorty nodded. Wolf Nelson closed his mouth.

"Dancin' Warrior come in early this mornin'. Claimed he'd seen the paint's tracks way t-hell-an'-gone north of Rafter V."

"How could he tell for sure?" Shorty asked.

"Off-front shoe had a split caulk. Accordin' to Dancin' Warrior, tracks turned up a canyon."

"I'm scared," old Wolf said.

All eyes went on the wolfer. "Why'd you say that?" Sheriff Watson asked.

"I'm afraid they'll kill me!"

"Who'll kill you?"

Shorty said, "Go ahead an' talk, Wolf."

Wolf Nelson talked.

Chapter Seventeen

Had it not been for the buzzards, Dee Bowden undoubtedly would not have discovered the two dead horses. Had it not been so close to snowfall he'd have paid the circling vultures small attention, for usually buzzards had deserted this area by this time of the year.

The turkey buzzards circled west about half a mile. Occasionally one flew out of formation to land stiff-legged in the sagebrush, huge wings spread to break his descent.

Dee stood on stirrups, trying to see what they were eating, but the sagebrush was too high—it hid the dead animal.

Dee settled back in the Hamley, frowning. He'd not seen a four-legged animal except Jones since encountering the brockle-faced cow yesterday. Were the vultures picking the bones of a dead coyote or lobo wolf, one killed in a fight or who had succumbed to old age?

Curiosity held him. He rode west. Here a canyon petered out, losing its identity on the rock-strewn plain. He had been wrong. The buzzards had not landed on the plain. They had sailed down into the canyon.

Wind savagely whipped in. It was so strong it even threw small pebbles around. It brought the stench of death. Dee rode into the canyon's end, gradually working downward. The stench grew stronger. He rounded a gravel wash. He glanced behind. Wind had already begun to whip clean the hoof prints of Jones, it was that strong.

Then, he came upon the first dead horse.

He circled to the north to rein in, astonishment strong—for the shot animal was Nancy Craig's pinto.

He read the Rafter V brand on the pinto's left shoulder. The horse had no saddle or bridle. He had been shot between the eyes. The buzzards had been eating him, long black beaks tearing.

He stared. Could he believe his eyes? He had to. There was the Rafter V brand, staring back.

The pinto was Nancy's favorite. He'd been orphaned by a late blizzard. Nancy had raised him on the bottle. He was always in the barn or on pasture. And now here he was dead— Miles from nowhere—

A cold hand gripped Dee's heart. Nancy would never have allowed the pinto to stray. And if he had broken from pasture he'd not have strayed this far. Logic told him Nancy had ridden him here.

Then where was Nancy?

Sitting there, cold wind shipping in, Dee Bowden realized he loved Nancy Craig. He had suspected such before. Now he was sure. And fear for her safety tore at his young heart.

Suddenly, Millie didn't count. Up to now, he'd been undetermined. Now he was sure.

He rode in a circle, searching for tracks. Wind bent sagebrush and greasewood almost double. Sand flew. The gale screamed in the pines. He rode closer to the canyon's south wall. There he caught the hoof prints of cattle, for here the wind could not whip in.

His scowl deepened. Why had cattle moved through here? The answer was simplicity itself. The cattle had been stolen. Rustled. And Nancy somehow had fallen into the hands of the rustlers!

He gave the scene a last glance, realizing there was nothing he could do here—and then he caught the stench of something dead down-canyon.

Buzzards circled there, too.

He rode a quarter-mile and came upon a dead roan horse, buzzards lifting as Jones and he approached. His astonishment grew. Banker John Hendricks' roan stud!

He wasn't sure. There were lots of roans on Round Rock range, both strawberry and blue. The horse lay on his right side, forelegs extended. Dee could read no brand.

Evidently the brand was on the right side of the animal. Dee knew it bore a Colorado iron, N Bar S. He shook down his lasso. He roped the extended forelegs and with Jones leaning hard against the cinch he turned the horse over.

The N Bar S stood out clearly on the roan's flank. The roan had been shot in the forehead.

Why had the horses been killed?

Dee could only guess. The pinto was too showy, too gaudy. He immediately attracted attention. Therefore his rider too would attract attention.

But the roan—

Dee then noticed that one of the roan's forelegs was out of kilter. It hung in an odd manner. He knew then why the roan had been destroyed.

He turned Jones west. Soon he was back on the rock-rimmed plains again, the full force of the cold autumn wind hammering him. He judged himself and horse some forty odd miles from Golden Gulch.

His surprise had changed to anger. Common sense told him Nancy was a captive of the Golden Gulch rustlers. He was half the distance to the mining camp which now contained around ten thousand people, he had heard.

Golden Gulch presented a big market for beef. Stolen beef. And, from what he had heard, more gold-crazy miners swarmed each day into the placer-mine area.

Dee did not know that behind him thundered Sheriff Isaac Watson with trailing mustaches, riding one tough horse and leading another. And with the lawman rode Shorty Messenger, armed and angry, with Mack Weston driving hard on Shorty's right, he also riding a tough horse and leading another.

A few paces behind was burly Jim North, hunched in Furstnow saddle against the cold wind. Then came five townsmen, hard-fighting, hard-riding men all, and each rider led an extra mount.

Every half hour they changed mounts. They reined to jarring halts, shod hoofs digging sand and gravel. They hit the ground before their saddle-horses were actually stopped.

High heels dug for purchase. Saddles were quickly pulled free, latigo straps singing as they slipped from cinch rings. Not a man guided his bronc by a bridle. All horses had only hackamores, rawhide-braided bosals riding just above open, expanded nostrils.

Thus, there were no bridles to change. And each horse breathed more easily without steel in his mouth.

Old Wolf Nelson brought up the rear. He had demanded to go along. His mules had been too slow. Somebody had loaned him two stout, fast horses. He rode bareback, brandishing a Winchester rifle.

Behind him and around him loped his hounds, tongues dragging. Occasionally the hounds darted aside to run down and kill a coyote. They hit the unfortunate coyote on the run, the bitch hound starting the attack by lunging in and toppling the tired wilding.

"Danged fool of a kid," Sheriff Watson grumbled as he hurriedly smoothed his Navajo saddle-blanket over the back of his spare bronc. "Why didn't he come to me with his story, 'cause I'm the law."

Shorty Messenger slung his Cheyenne kak over his saddle-blanket. "Don't tickle me to death, sher'ff. This ain't my day to die laughin'. If Dee'd come to you you'd have jugged him an' you know it."

"Guess I would, with what little I knew then. You boys all set to ride ag'in?"

All were now mounted except Wolf Nelson who, although he had no saddle, was having a tough time mounting because of his rifle. The others packed their rifles in saddle-boots.

Jim North rode close. "Gimme thet rifle an' I'll jam it down alongside of mine in my scabbard."

"No—"

"Dang it, you're holdin' up the parade, wolfer! Gimme it or I'll climb off'n this cayuse and beat the daylights outa you!"

"You touch me," Wolf said, "an' I'll git my friend Shorty to beat the bull outa you!"

"Shorty an' me have buried the hatchet—an' not in the other man's skull, either. Someday I aim to show him he caught me by su'prise an' that I can whup him but thet ain't here or now."

"He sure handed yuh a big black eye an—"

North tore the Winchester from the wolfer's dirty hands. He jammed it barrel-down into his saddle-boot over his own rifle. "Now get on thet cayuse, wolfer—an' ride! An' why didn't you get a saddle in town afore we started out?"

"I likes to feel my bronc under my laigs an' not a hunk of leather." Wolf Nelson swung up onto his horse. "Okay, cowboys—let's ride hell fer leather!"

"We ride," Sheriff Watson tersely said.

Night came rapidly down. The wind's coldness increased. Horses galloped on, hoofs clashing gravel to send out sparks from horseshoes.

There was no moon. Only high Wyoming starlight lighting the ghostly terrain, throwing sagebrush and greasewood into eerie relief.

They changed horses. Each horse was given a measure of water taken from each Sioux water-bag, the steer gut. Old Wolf Nelson had had the presence of mind to take along a small bucket.

A horse had just room enough in the bucket to insert his nose. Each saddle-bag carried a measure of oats mingled in with cartridges. Each man ate of pemmican or beef jerky.

There was no moon. Only the dim and cold stars. Dawn was slow in coming. Shorty Messenger suddenly

155

reined in his mount. Others drew rein. Shorty said, "There's a dead animal aroun' somewhere."

Old Wolf sniffed. "Horse stink, men. Not a dead cow, but a horse. I know."

Sheriff Watson said, "What'd a horse or cow be doin' here on this god-forsaken mesa?"

Old Wolf said, "Look-see my houn's!"

The hounds were running due east. By the time the posse had arrived the hungry dogs were tearing putrid flesh from the dead pinto and Hendricks' dead roan stud.

They rode around the dead animals. Daylight had seeped in enough to show brands on the two dead horses.

"Thet roan is Hendricks' hoss," the sheriff said. "Me, this I don't understan'. We're way north. Hendricks was seen ridin' south."

"A man can always neckrein a bronc a different direction," Shorty Messenger said. "Thet other— That's Nancy's pinto."

"Thet stud was a-layin' on his other side," a posseman said, "an' somebody's roped his front legs an' rolled him over. You can see the marks left in the sand."

"N Bar S iron," another man said. "That's the bran' Hendricks' stud packed. Done heard it was a Colorady iron."

"Rafter V wire-branded on the left shoulder," Shorty said. "That's Nancy's pinto. Both hosses been shot through the head."

Suddenly, the full implication created by the two dead horses hit the riders. They stared from one to the other in amazement and fear, dawn etching the deep lines of their tired faces.

Sheriff Isaac Watson slowly said, "I wish I was a prayin' man but I ain't. We jes' got to hope fer the best. Thet roan stud—somethin' was wrong with his off-front laig— But the pinto looks to me like he wasn't lame or had a busted leg—"

"Same to me," Shorty Messenger said.

Sheriff Watson stood high on stirrups and looked at

the ground for sign. "Win's blowed everythin' away. Covered all tracks with sand. Mind we ride in a circle, mebbe we'll fin' somethin'?"

They circled. They discovered the hoof-tracks of cattle in the sheltered area where but a few hours before Dee Bowden had ridden. Sheriff Watson rocked in his Malta rig, hands locked around the horn, and he seriously said, "There was a big herd of cattle moved through here just lately. So many they filled this draw an' was crowded ag'in the sides of this draw."

"Headin' up canyon," Shorty Messenger said. "Look, here's tracks of a hoss—wearin' shoes, too. Shoes tell us somebody rid him."

Behind them, hounds tore at horse flesh.

"How would dogies get up on this god-forsaken mesa?" a townsman asked. All eyes turned on Jim North, who had ridden Round Rock range from the Montana border to the Big Horn.

"They'd have to come up the canyon where the Shoshoni saw the hoofprints of Nancy's pinto. Then over a ridge and down into what is called Hell Gate Canyon."

"Am' where does Hell Gate lead to?" the sheriff asked.

"Straight to a hell named Golden Gulch. Runs right through town but not very deep there. In fact, some placer mines are in Hell Gate Canyon."

Shorty Messenger remembered hearing that Jim North had two months ago ridden to Golden Gulch, thinking he'd placer mine. He'd soon discovered a shovel did not fit his hands as did a lass-rope and had soon returned.

They rode northwest. They came to the dividing area between the two canyons. The wind had died now. All was calm. Here there was no wind when the sun rose or when the sun set. Nobody could explain this phenomenon. Nature just played in that manner.

Without wind, mosquitos swarmed in by the millions. You could hear them coming. They instantly attacked man and beast alike. The horses had it the worse, though—small gray deer-flies and big green horse-flies appeared out of nowhere and when they bit a horse they left a welt behind in his tight hide.

"Hit the trail, men," Sheriff Watson ordered.

They thundered across the wide desolation, but the mosquitos and flies kept happy pace. Within ten minutes the wind resumed blowing. It howled and danced and threw sand and small pebbles gleefully into the air.

The posse slowed down. "Wonder where them mosquitoes come from?" a man said. "The closest water is at least ten miles—if not more—away."

"How far to the beginin's of Hell Gate Canyon?" Sheriff Watson shot the question to Jim North.

"I was lucky Dee Bowden didn't kill me back in Tanner's Canyon," the townsman said. "He could have. I was out in the open. He spared my life. I'll repay him if I can."

"I didn't ask you about you an' Dee," the sheriff hollered. "I asked how far about to Hell Gate Canyon?"

Jim North looked about. "I'd say twenty miles, mebbe a few less. Dang, if there wasn't no wind a man couldn't live in this country. "Squitters'd eat him an' his an' livestock to death."

"Wind sure blewed them away," Shorty Messenger said.

Grim-faced, they loped on.

Chapter Eighteen

Dee Bowden's horse was leg-weary. Mark Stratton changed horses every ten miles. Dee had to rest Jones during each night. Stratton could ride all night. Thus on the evening of the second day out Mark Stratton caught up with Dee Bowden.

Dee had five thousand dollars on his head. He not only watched the area ahead and on all sides but also behind. Therefore he glimpsed the oncoming, hard-riding saloon-keeper.

Dee looked for a place to hole up for the night. He judged himself to be about eight miles out of Golden Gulch. He planned to ride into the gold-mad town in the morning.

Nancy Craig was in danger. Even now she might have been killed. He would give himself up to the Golden Gulch sheriff. He'd tell the sheriff all he knew. From then on it would be in the hands of the law.

And he'd be in Golden Gulch jail.

Here the terrain consisted of scarp hills and deep canyons, for ahead were the Grand Tetons. Dee rode ridges. Thus pine hid him as he drew rein and focused his glasses on the fast-riding newcomer.

Night was swiftly dropping but there was still enough daylight to identify Mark Stratton. Dee watched until the man rode below him on the trail some two hundred yards below.

Stratton had a sack tied behind his saddle's cantle. Even at this distance Dee noticed it seemed rather full. Evidently grub and other supplies, the wanted cowboy deducted.

Dee tried to add up points. Ahead of him was a herd of stolen Round Rock cattle, banker John Hendricks and rustlers—yes, and captive Nancy Craig. And now here was the saloon-keeper, Mark Stratton.

Stratton plainly rode to join Hendricks?

Dee Bowden did some mental arithmetic. A year ago Stratton and Hendricks had arrived in Round Rock at about the same time. Did that signify anything?

Had these two known each other before Round Rock?

Dee Bowden restored his glasses to their case. He laid his hand on the stock of his Winchester. It would be a simple and easy shot to shoot the horse from under Stratton.

He'd then make Stratton talk. If the saloon-keeper didn't want to talk, he'd get the heat treatment he'd given old Wolf Nelson. The burn-treatment Byers had received, also.

But Dee Bowden let Stratton ride past unmolested. He knew he could not trail the man for night was too close. You can't trail in darkness.

Dee decided to ride into Golden Gulch in the morning. Or maybe even later on, after Jones had had a brief rest.

There he'd give himself up to the Golden Gulch sheriff. He'd tell the sheriff that Nancy Craig was missing and that he feared her kidnapped and moving with a stolen herd of Round Rock basin cattle.

The sheriff would jail him, of course—but he'd be safe in Golden Gulch's jail. Nobody in Golden Gulch except the Golden Gulch law would give a rap about what had happened in Round Rock.

No Golden Gulch lynch-mob would storm him in jail.

First, he had to rest Jones. Accordingly, he stripped saddle, blanket and bridle from the tough cayuse.

A little grass grew in the pines. The pines had held

water from running-off. He put Jones on the end of his lass-rope as a picket-rope. Jones immediately began cropping grass.

Dee sat at the edge of the pines. Night fell; stars played. He was very, very tired. He slipped into a broken sleep.

He dreamed a posse closed in, rifles snarling. And Jones— Jones was so leg-tired Jones stumbled, fell— And a bullet—

Dee Bowden jerked awake, hand on his Winchester beside him. The night had grown cold.

He heard hoofs approaching from the southeast. He became instantly alert. A group of riders approached. Starlight did not allow for recognition, but voices came clearly across the Wyoming crispness.

"We ain't too far from Golden Gulch, men."

Dee became completely awake. Unless he was dead wrong, that squeaky voice could belong to only one person—Sheriff Isaac Watson.

Watson led a posse hunting him. Then Dee heard another masculine voice say, "I wonder where t'heck Dee is located?"

Shorty Messenger's long-familiar voice!

"Wish we could fin' Dee." Sheriff Watson's voice.

Then Shorty again with, "Hope nothin' serious has happened to him."

The riders moved past out of voice-range. They loped into the starlight and became lost in the distance as they rode toward Golden Gulch. Finally distance killed even the sound of their hoofs.

Dee Bowden scratched his head, frowning deeply.

What in tarnation did a Round Rock posse do in this faraway area? Sheriff Watson and his men were far beyond the limits of the sheriff's bailiwick.

Which did the sheriff trail—stolen cattle or Dee Bowden? Dee wished he knew, for sure....

He got to his feet. He recalled the few words he'd heard. Plainly, Sheriff Watson searched for him, Dee Bowden. Watson had said so. But yet—

Shorty Messenger's words— Shorty was his best friend. And here Shorty rode with a posse searching for him.

Dee slowly shook his head, shaking away all sleep. Shorty would never ride out to gun-down his best friend. Dee suddenly realized the posse was hunting him, yes— but not to kill him. Shorty's words were the key-words.

Something serious had happened in Round Rock. Dee was sure one of the riders had been old Wolf Nelson. Now all was clear, plain. Wolf had told Sheriff Watson what he knew. This had involved Mark Stratton. And Stratton had fled Round Rock.

Within minutes, he was in leather, riding the high ridges as hard as tired Jones could run, but the posse kept ahead. He caught the Round Rock riders when they stopped to change broncs.

By pure happenstance, Sheriff Isaac Watson was the closest to him. He jammed the barrel of the rifle against the lawman's spine. Watson jumped in surprise, then steadied when Dee said, "Dee Bowden, here. I don't know why you ride, Round Rock men—but I'm takin' no chances of bein' a hangtree's fruit!"

Watson put his hands high. The others turned, stared, hardly believing their eyes. Jim North said, "By hell, it is Dee!"

Shorty Messenger said, "We come lookin' for you, Dee, but not to hang you. We come to tell you that ol' Wolf saw Byers kill Branch Craig."

"You're innocent," Sheriff Watson said.

Dee studied each face as well as he could under the uncertain starlight. Was this a ruse to get him to lower his rifle? So they could leap on him and bear him to the ground?

It was Shorty Messenger who made up Dee Bowden's decision. Shorty said, "Dee, I'd never ride to hang you— an' you know that, pal."

Dee's throat clogged. He was again a free man. He stood frozen, hardly believing, and Sheriff Watson said,

"I'm danged tired of havin' my hands up high like this, Bowden."

Dee's rifle dropped. "Nancy Craig?"

"Far as we can deduct from thet dead pinto she's behin' held by the rustlers," Sheriff Watson said. "Only thing we could read into that sign. You know anythin' about her?"

"Nothin' certain. Only I read sign like you do."

Shorty Messenger said, "Your hunch about ol' Wolf was right, Dee. He admits he aimed to rob Branch Craig but claims he'd not have killed Craig, jus' hit him from behin' an' taken him to the groun' an' robbed him—Craig was that drunk."

"I know where Byers buried Craig's money in Devil's Canyon," old Wolf Nelson said. "Stratton done pulled outa Round Rock, Dee."

Dee said, "He rode past about two hours ago, maybe less."

Sheriff Isaac Watson said, "He's goin' join Hendricks. Them two has been bossin' this rustlin'. I'd've looked into this long time ago but Branch Craig—Hell, he was so drunk all the time a man doubted his word!"

They told about the Round Rock bank being robbed, the old bookkeeper murdered. "Things point to Stratton," Shorty said. "With him in cahoots with Hendricks, we figure he had a key to the bank—'cause the door wasn't jimmied. Been opened by a key."

Jim North had walked about, occasionally kneeling. Now he said, "Cow tracks all over. Headed toward Golden Gulch. Pancakes just a few hours old. How about notifyin' the law in Golden Gulch, sher'ff?"

Sheriff Watson snorted. "Kill that idea, North. Sher'ff Johson is as crooked as a garter-snake. He's a politician and he has his hand out to be greased all the time. Me, I figure he's gettin' paid under the table, so much a head of russled Round Rock beef!"

"Then it's up to us alone," Shorty said.

Dee Bowden walked to a nearby huge sandstone. He leaned against it, still stunned. All the time drunken Wolf

163

Nelson had known he had not killed Branch Craig.

"I oughta choke you to death, Wolf."

Wolf Nelson said, "I don't blame you, Bowden." He laughed drunkenly. "But I'm thankful to Hank Byers. I might've killed Branch Craig to git that money. Byers might've saved me from a noose!"

"Why didn't you tell this at the coroner's inquest?" Dee demanded.

"I was ascared thet if I talked somebody'd kill me for blabbin'," the wolfer said. "An I—"

Sheriff Watson cut in with, "Enough of such blabbin', men. We gotta fin' the slaughter grounds fast 'cause I think them stolen Round Rock cows'll be hangin' as beef from hooks soon."

All eyes swung to the sheriff, who suddenly seemed to gain character and stature.

"Jim North, you an' Slim scout in Golden Gulch. I'm knowed there so if I rode in everybody'd figger somethin' had brought me to this area, so I'll wait here."

Jim North and Slim Westrum nodded.

Sheriff Watson spoke to Shorty and Dee Bowden. "You two ride ahead. Fin' where the herd is located. Then head back here pronto."

"What about Nancy?" Dee asked.

The sheriff tugged his left mustache. "Try to locate her, too. An' let's all pray to God she ain't been harmed . . . or kilt to silence her."

Round Rock men, rifles in hand, went to horses.

Chapter Nineteen

Stratton knew where the beeves would be slaughtered. He had ridden this rustler-trail a few times. Two miles southeast of Golden Gulch the herd of three hundred head were pointed up an angling trail leading to the southern rim of Hell Gate Canyon.

Cattle were scrambling up this trail when he rode upon banker John Hendricks, who guarded the rear. Very little starlight penetrated this deep abyss but Stratton heard the rasp of cloven hoofs on igneous rock as he neared the herd.

"Round Rock ridin' in," he called, reining in his saddler.

He got no answer. Just the sounds of hoofs. The wind came in, bringing the scent of sweaty horses and bovines.

Agin he called, "Round Rock ridin' in!"

This time a voice called, "Ride in, Round Rock."

Stratton grinned. He recognized John Hendricks' voice. Hendricks pulled in a bit-fighting bay. "What're you doin' out here, Mark?"

"The whole thing blew up. Wolf Nelson talked."

Hendricks sat saddle for a long moment and then said, "The money in my bank?"

"Tied behin' my saddle. I had an extra key, remember. I robbed the bank two mornin's ago, early. Left the silver behin' an' took all paper money."

Hendricks nodded. "Not much hard silver there. You get the gold?"

"I got it." Stratton hesitated, then said, "The old cashier— He caught me— Ol' Sig Livingston—"

"Yeah?"

"I had to kill him."

Hendricks said, "Another murder charge means nothin'. Anybody see you leave?"

"I dunno. Some people in Round Rock get up early. Some might stay up all night. I rode south until I got to Elkhorn crick. Then I rode up it an' headed this direction. Nancy Craig's missin'."

Hendricks said, "She came snoopin' behind us. We had to grab her to keep her from ridin' back an' talkin'."

Stratton's brows rose. "Where is she now?"

"Tied to her hoss at the head of the herd."

"What do you aim to do with her?" .

Hendricks shrugged thin shoulders. "I don't know. I believe it's best we leave that up to Cy."

"Cy? Hell, he's a killer. All killer. He'll murder her."

"What would be wrong with that?"

Stratton moved in saddle. "Like you said, what's another murder. Let's chouse these damn bossies up this hill. Anybody ride into Golden Gulch fer the cow-buyer?"

"Lee Underwood rode in. Left the herd back in the canyon. Butcher and his gang—and knives—should be waiting. Whit Patterson rode in with Underwood."

"Then we ride out."

"We ride out," Hendricks assured. "Headin' south with two extra broncs an' not one. We gotta cover ground, Mark."

"An' fast," Stratton said.

Stratton uncoiled his lass-rope from his saddle-fork. He began beating stolen beef over the back to force the reluctant cattle to climb the trail faster.

Cows bawled. Steers climbed, hoofs slipping. Starlight showed a sinuous line of beeves climbing out of Hell Gage Canyon. Time was the essence. Stratton knew this; so did Hendricks.

"The herd left tracks," Stratton hollered. "I saw them.

166

Why didn't you stick to the lava beds with them?"

"We're in cow country now," Hendricks corrected. "Big cow-outfits aroun' here— N Bar Six. Chimney Top. A Lazy V Bar. Those outfits move cattle along here. All cows leave the same droppin's."

Stratton whacked a steer over the rump with his doubled manila. The longhorn whirled, charged. Stratton's horse, used to working ornery steers, leaped aside. The steer thundered past, skidded to a halt, swung back and charged again.

Hendricks roweled his cutting-horse forward. The saddle horse's shoulder hit the steer's shoulder with a resounding whack. The boogery steer was thrown off stride.

The steer stumbled over a trampled brush. He went sliding down on his throat, rasping hide from his under-jaw. He scrambled up, fight gone. Desperately, hoofs digging, he began to climb.

Stratton felt a sense of freedom. He was again a Texan, working cattle. Stink of manure. The bawl of a cow. The angry bellow of a bull. And over it all the smell and the dust and a horse under your legs working stock, moving here, heading off here.

"I gave my saloon to Pancho," he hollered to Hendricks. "I put him in charge. You should have seen him swell up, Twice his normal size. He doesn't know yet it's his saloon, but it is."

Hendricks said, "T'hell with a bank. I had too much of that. Only good thing about it was the money."

"Money's the only good thing about anything," Stratton said.

Henricks turned his bronc on the horse's hind legs, rifle brandished. "I'm ridin' back to check the backtrail. A man never knows...."

"That's right. I'll put these cows up the hill. When I call out, you'll know they're all climbin'."

Hendricks turned his bronc. He melted into the starlighted brush. Stratton pounded a cow over the back,

167

remembering that Hendricks had not asked him about Craig's money buried in Devil's Canyon.

Stratton wished he had that money.

Quite a sum.... Wolf Nelson would lead Sheriff Watson to it, undoubtedly. Or Wolf would play it foxy. He'd dig here and there and then claim he did not know exactly where the money was buried. That his memory failed him due to age, or some such thing.

Then Wolf might sneak back, dig up the money, and disappear. Stratton allowed himself a small smile. He might even run across Wolf Nelson down in southern California?

Old Wolf was nobody's fool. Drunkard, alcoholic, yeah—but far from stupid.

He hadn't asked Hendricks about the roan stud, either. His horse turned sharply, cut back a bunch-quitter; soon, the last stolen beef had his hoofs scrambling up the up-hill trail.

Stratton pulled in his sweating horse. He cupped big hands to his mouth. "Round Rock," he called.

He got no answer.

He waited a long moment, then called again. Again, no answer. He scowled and admitted to himself he was afraid. On this grass they hanged cowthieves, as Craig had told Bowden.

"Round Rock."

Brush crackled at his left. Hurriedly, he jerked his bronc around, gun rising from holster.

The gun came half-out, hesitated, dropped—for the rider was John Hendricks, .25-35 rifle in hand. "All headed up, huh?"

"All climbin', John."

Stratton's horses began climbing, Hendricks' saddler following. They finally reached the brush-covered summit. Stratton glimpsed the snow-covered Tetons, dim to the northwest.

Sagebrush here grew as tall as a tall horse. The stolen herd now moved due west. Golden Gulch's lamps were now northwest.

Cattle were boogery. Steers moved hurriedly, jerkily. They grabbed at bunchgrass.

Rifle across saddle, Hendricks rode drag. Other rustlers rode the flanks, lass-ropes beating. Cyrus Zachary rode point. He sent a rustler a quarter-mile ahead.

"Jake, scare the coyotes—or jackrabbits—out of the way. These cattle are ready to stampede. Just a rabbit leapin' up—"

"An' they'd be on their way," Jake said, loping ahead.

Cattle kept moving, bawling, hooking horns, mounting the other. Finally Golden Gulch's lights were straight north. Slowly, the herd wound on through the high sagebrush until finally the gold-mad town's lights were to the northeast.

Here lay a half-mile-wide natural bowl in the foothills. Cattle began descending a narrow trail downward. This was the kill-area. Here was a large pine-pole corral and here would be the scaffolding on which the cattle would be hung to be skinned and become dressed beeves.

Zachary and Stratton and Hendricks galloped toward the corral. Here sagebrush grew exceptionally high. Cattle moved no more than two abreast, sagebrush almost hiding them.

Stratton figured the cow-buyer would await the herd at the corral. Usually the cattle were counted by Hendricks and the buyer as they filed into the corral area.

The buyer's crew skinned and dressed the beef. Usually this crew consisted of at least twenty men.

But nobody awaited at the corral.

Stratton said, "You said you sent a man in to get the buyer, Cy?"

"I did, Mark."

Hendricks said, "I don't understan' this. Usually that damned cow-thief of a buyer is out here ahead of time."

A rustler rode up leading Nancy Craig's horse with Nancy's hands tied to the saddle's horn. "What will I do with the woman?" He spoke to Hendricks.

Twenty yards north, at the edge of the high sagebrush,

was a sod one-room shack, its backside built into a rocky hill. "Put her in there," Hendricks said.

Cattle grouped around the corral's outside. There was no use corraling them. They'd have to be only driven out when the buyer arrived and then driven in with the buyer and Hendricks sitting beside the corral gate making a count as the dogies entered.

Time ran by. Still, no buyer, no kill-crew. Cattle became more restless. Steers pawed dust, horns clashed, horns locked other horns. Raw impatience held the rustlers.

Hendricks sent out two rustlers to see if the buyer and crew were in sight. The two men rode up the northern hill and out of sight. Hendricks looked at Stratton.

"You're shiverin'," the banker said. "'Scared?"

Stratton glanced at his long-time companion. Hendricks' voice had held an undertone. "Cold night," Stratton clipped.

Hendricks laughed silently.

Stratton angrily said, "You son-of-a—" He suddenly clipped his sentence short, staring at the northern slope. "What the hell is comin' off now?"

For three riders had materialized out of starlight. They galloped down the hill to where the rustlers waited.

Two horsemen were the rustlers Hendricks had sent out. The center rider was one of the buyer's crew.

"They cut us off, Hendricks. Came between us an' the herd—"

"Who did?" Savagely, tersely.

"Don't know who t'hell they was! They come in with rifles an' sixguns. They pistol-whipped York—!"

"York was the cow-buyer.

"They pistol-whipped the rest, too. York an' the boys were lucky to escape alive—"

"Where's York now?" Hendricks demanded.

"Rode back to town. I managed to escape— There'll be no kill tonight— God almighty, my haid! A small guy hammered me down— Long mustaches—"

170

"Mustaches?" Stratton asked.

"Yeah, big ones. I've never seen him afore but he said he was a sher'ff—"

Hendricks looked at Stratton. Hendricks looked at Zachary. "Nobody but Sheriff Watson from Round Rock. An'—"

Hendricks never completed his sentence. Stratton cut in with, "Look-see to the west, men. Look at that fire—"

His words were drowned by a mighty roar. All along the western rim of the sagebrush-filled basin naked red flame shot upward following strong explosions throwing up boulders and earth.

"Dynamite!" Cy Zachary screamed.

For one red long second all hung in suspended animation. Flame and roar pounded across sagebrush. Immediately, tall sagebrush burst into roaring flame.

The harsh ever-present wind swept in, sweeping the fire. Dry sagebrush responded with alacrity.

The herd stood petrified for one moment. Then, with a bawl and clash of horns, the cattle stampeded.

"Ride out!" Stratton screamed.

His words were wasted. Already Zachary and Hendricks had spurred forward. Riding high on oxbows, Stratton's mount plunged after the two, eyes wide and red in the reflected flames.

All was confusion. Cloven hoofs smashed down sagebrush. The corral, sturdy as it was, went down, timbers flying all directions. Steers bawled. Cows went berserk.

Wind whipped the flames in a crown-fire that traveled across the top of the dried sagebrush. Within a few minutes the fire was beating the drag steers on their rumps.

A steer stumbled, fell, tried to struggle up, but fire swept over him, and he went down again, flame searing his lungs. Stratton, quirting his bronc, glanced back, leaned in saddle and screamed to Hendricks, "They're gainin', John!"

171

Hendricks yelled, "Bowden! Dee Bowden! He's behin—" The roar of wild hoofs and crackling flames killed the rest of his words.

Horses stretched out, running madly, riders quirting and spurring. A horse stumbled over a sagebrush root, throwing his rider. Instantly crown-flame claimed rustler and cayuse.

The man got to his boots, tried to run, but fire caught his clothing, making him a flaming torch. He went down, screaming. Fire swept over him. His horse did not even get a chance to try to rise.

Now a running steer was abreast of Stratton's bronc, the last horse in the race for the hills. Turning on stirrups, Stratton's .45 lifted, spouted smoke.

The steer went down. Hoofs pounded into him, reducing him to mere flesh within a minute. A cow stumbled, piled up, didn't rise.

Stratton straightened in saddle. His .45 had given him a little more time. His quirt rose, fell. His bloodshot eyes searched the hills ahead. Would they never reach them? Pine trees there offered protection.

Smoke swept in. Stratton coughed hackingly. Gray smoke covered the basin, hiding the last steers in the stampede.

The hills came closer. Suddenly, Hendricks' mount faltered, stumbled, fell. Hendricks was thrown from saddle. Stratton thundered past, nearly colliding with Hendricks' horse as the horse struggled to his hoofs.

Hendricks began to run. He screamed something unintelligible as Stratton galloped madly past. Stratton glanced back. His blood changed to ice-water.

For a steer hit Hendricks with his horns. The man went reeling. Another steer smashed into the banker. Hendricks went to the ground. Stratton never saw him again. Cattle pounded over Hendricks.

Hendricks' horse also went down under the wild hoofs. Stratton gave his attention to his laboring mount. The horse was weary. He'd traveled far and now this stampede—

"Look ahead!" screamed Cy Zachary.

Six riders rimmed the hill ahead. Zachary's rifle lifted and he shot from the saddle. Gunfire blossomed on the hill's rim. Horses reared and fought bits. Gunsmoke rolled in. Stratton gained the hills. A great relief entered him. Here in the pines he was safe and could make his escape.

Gunfire roared behind him. Sixshooters belched flame. Rifles spat whining bullets. His mind settled. He would escape. Zachary was dead. He dimly remembered Zachary pitching from saddle, Zachary's rifle skidding ahead of Zachary's falling body.

Zachary hadn't moved.

Stratton spurred south. He followed a trail made by deer and elk and bear. Pines hid him. The sound of gunfire died behind. No longer did he hear the crackle of flames. His blood sang. He was making good his escape.

Now no prison sentence loomed ahead. He had a sackful of money tied behind his saddle. Now all that money was his. He added points.

A posse had ridden out from Round Rock. Sheriff Isaac Watson had headed it. The posse had swung into Golden Gulch. There the posse had bought dynamite. It was easy to get dynamite in Golden Gulch.

Golden Gulch was a mining town. Mining towns depended on dynamite for their livelihoods. Dynamite blasted loose rock and gravel that held gold.

Stratton's horse thundered into a wide clearing. Then it was that the saloon-keeper head a woman scream, "Dee Bowde, come back here, please!"

He recognized Nancy Craig's voice. The posse had freed Nancy. And Nancy called to Dee Bowden. That meant Bowden was somewhere around and—

Suddenly, a horseman blocked the trail ahead. Mark Stratton pulled his plunging mount in, hand going to his holstered gun. He stopped ten yards away from the silent horseman.

Starlight washed across the dried grass of the mountain park. Starlight glistened on silver-mounted bits

173

and spurs. Starlight showed the faces of each man clearly.

Dee Bowden said, "That's far enough, Stratton."

Stratton remembered Dee Bowden drawing against Branch Craig in the Diamond Willow. Craig had been slow, in his estimation, but Bowden had been dog-slow.

Mark Stratton was himself, now. Once again he was the cold-blooded gambler who sat emotionless and dead-pan.

His eyes took in salient points. Dee Bowden had his .45 in holster. His right hand rested on the gun's grip.

Stratton's .45 also was leathered. He'd automatically put his palm on its bone handle when reining in.

He and Dee Bowden were even-up. Now the draw of the gun counted. And again he remembered Dee Bowden's slowness.

Stratton thought, *All odds favor me.*

He then remembered Nancy Craig's cry. Nancy Craig was somewhere to his right in the timber. Maybe the odds didn't favor him? Maybe even now Nancy Craig had a rifle—or pistol—on him from concealment?

Now he heard a horse threshing through brush to the right. That told him Nancy Craig rode and did not sit a motionless horse.

Nancy Craig called, "Dee, where are you?"

Dee Bowden paid her call no attention. He said, "Are you comin' peaceful or do I have to force you, Stratton?"

Stratton threw back his heavy head, starlight shimmering on the silver buckle of his hat-band. Stratton said, "You'll have to force me, Bowden," and he made his draw.

Swiftly his .45 rose, brushing greased leather. He saw he was way ahead of Dee Bowden. He would kill Bowden. Savage fire licked through Stratton's pounding arteries.

He fired from the hip. He'd spent hours practicing that hip-shot. But practice was not reality—a tin-can was not a man who aimed to kill you before you killed him.

And Stratton shot too fast. And Mark Stratton missed.

Surprise surged through him. He had missed a sure

174

shot. Surprise changed to anger.

He, a professional gambler, had taken an unnecessary gamble—and lost. He'd had plenty of time to lift, level, aim—and shoot.

He'd lift now. His gun started up—

Something smashed into his chest. The blow drove him from saddle. He landed sitting on pine needles.

His terrified horse ran away, reins trailing.

Stratton's gun flew from his grip to land fifteen feet away. Blood colored his fancy brocaded vest. Stratton's head went down. He stared at the redness.

Heart pounding, Dee Bowden dismounted, warily watching.

Stratton lifted his head. He stared at his gun. He seemed to be measuring the distance between himself and the weapon.

With supreme effort, he got on hands and knees. Slowly, carefully, breathing heavily, he began creeping toward the .45.

Five feet from the pistol, he stopped and his right hand began groping, fingers feeling, digging pine needles. He apparently couldn't see the weapon. His groping fingers searched.

Dee Bowden watched with a sickened heart. He had hoped to take Stratton alive. He had not wanted to kill Stratton. Never had he wanted to take the life of a fellow human.

Suddenly, Stratton rolled on his left side. He stared up at Dee. Dee was sure the man did not see him.

Stratton's lips moved. Slowly he said, "Anythin' is better than bars. . . ." He said no more.

He sighed deeply and lay still.

"Dee, where are you?"

"Over here, Nancy."

"Are you—all right?"

"Yes."

Dee put his head against Jones' sweaty shoulder. Stratton, he knew, was dead. No man could live with a bullet through his chest. Jones swung his head back and nuzzled Dee's shoulder.

Nancy Craig rode into the clearing. She drew rein. She looked at Stratton with horrified eyes, then slowly dismounted.

She went to Dee who still stood beside Jones.

"It's all over, Dee. When Hendricks went down the other rustlers gave up. Everybody is all right except Jim North—"

Dee remained silent.

"Jim got shot through the forearm. Bone isn't broken and Watson had bandages in his saddle-bag. The cattle are drifting back home and—"

"Hey, Dee! Where the hell are you?"

That was Shorty Messenger's voice. Dee lifted his head. Starlight showed the stark terror leaving his young face.

"Over here, Shorty."

"I'm comin' in, Dee!"

Horses trailing, Dee Bowden and Nancy Craig walked from the clearing, hand in hand.

High starlight glistened.